SEARCHER

JOSH EDWARDS

CHARTER/DIAMOND BOOKS, NEW YORK

SEARCHER

A Charter/Diamond Book / published by arrangement with
the author

PRINTING HISTORY
Charter/Diamond edition / August 1990

All rights reserved.
Copyright © 1990 by Charter Communications, Inc.
This book may not be reproduced in whole or in part, by
mimeograph or any other means, without permission.
For information address: The Berkley Publishing Group,
200 Madison Avenue, New York, New York 10016.

ISBN: 1-55773-307-4

Charter/Diamond Books are published by
The Berkley Publishing Group,
200 Madison Avenue, New York, New York 10016.
The name ''CHARTER/DIAMOND'' and its logo
are trademarks belonging to Charter Communications, Inc.

PRINTED IN THE UNITED STATES OF AMERICA

10   9   8   7   6   5   4   3   2   1

SEARCHER

1

Pouring sheets of rain whiplashed the main street of Crawford, Kansas. Wind rattled windows and whistled past storefronts, and not a soul was in sight. The middle of the street was a swamp.

A tall man appeared in the doorway of Gallagher's Stable. He wore a poncho and a big pearl-colored ex-Confederate cavalry officer's hat with the insignia torn off, and his pants were tucked into his boots cavalry style. He tightened the poncho around his neck and ran across the street, splashing water in all directions, tripping and nearly falling as his boot went into the muck up to his ankle.

He vaulted onto the boardwalk on the far side of the street in front of a sign that said:

SALOON

A roof over the boardwalk sheltered him from the rain, and he loosened the poncho around his neck, then pushed open the door and entered the saloon.

Several men stood at the bar. A few others sat at tables. It was a dark, dingy place, and a piano was in the corner, but nobody played. The wind howled outside on the street. He strolled to the bar.

"Whisky."

The bartender was also big, but thick around the middle, with a black handlebar mustache and long black sideburns. He placed a glass and a bottle of whisky on the bar in front of the newcomer.

All eyes were on him, and he was aware of their interest. He'd been on the frontier long enough to know that violence could break out at any moment in a small town saloon.

He poured some whisky into the glass and tossed it into his mouth. It burned all the way down, dispelling some of the chill in the air. A kerosene lamp was behind the bar near the cash register, casting its glow on the stranger's face. He had dark blond hair and steely blue eyes and his expression said: *Don't fuck with me*.

He poured himself another drink and gulped it down. The bartender washed a glass. The men in the saloon returned to their conversations, ignoring the stranger.

His name was John Stone, and he took off his hat, laying it on the bar. He pulled his poncho over his head, shaking it out on the floor and hanging it on a nearby hook. Underneath the poncho he wore a pale blue shirt and dark blue jeans. His Colt was slung low on his right side and tied to his leg. He put his hat back on and sat on the stool.

Cowboys laughed at a corner table. Stone sipped some whisky. This saloon looked like the one in the last town and the town before that. It had rough-hewn planked walls, a few racy pictures tacked up, a billiards table, and the head of a grizzly bear mounted above the bottles.

Stone opened his shirt pocket and took out a small photograph in a metal frame, covered with isinglass. It showed a young woman with blond hair wearing a party dress and looking to the side of the photographer.

"Bartender—ever see this woman?"

The bartender put on a pair of glasses and squinted at the photograph. "Can't say I have."

The bartender handed the photograph back, and Stone put it into his shirt pocket, buttoning the flap. He carried his bottle and glass to an empty table in a dark corner and sat down. Lightning flashed in the street outside, and a few seconds later a peal of thunder reverberated across the town.

Stone opened his other shirt pocket and took out a small leather tobacco pouch, rolled a cigarette, lit it, then leaned back in his chair. Rain pelted the windows of the bar, and thunder exploded overhead.

It reminded him of the war. During the Chambersburg Raid in October of 1862, he and his men had been soaked to the skin far behind Yankee lines at night, with stolen horses and supplies, and Yankee patrols were scouring the countryside for them.

He remembered the tension and discomfort, the feeling they weren't going to make it, but somehow they returned, and now scholars considered the Chambersburg Raid one of the most outstanding exploits in the history of cavalry.

Stone puffed his cigarette. Last he'd heard, Bobby Lee was president of Washington College. Wade Hampton was a politician back in South Carolina. Jeb Stuart was dead. The world he loved was gone forever, and all he had to show for it was an old faded picture in his shirt and a few coins in his jeans.

The saloon was half general store, and clothes hung from the rafters. Bags of beans and corn leaned against the walls. Three men played cards at the table nearest Stone. On the other side, a man was passed out cold. In the corner, an elderly man with a white mustache sat with a bottle and an old newspaper. A group of cowboys was at the bar.

Stone had run into many cowboys since coming to the frontier. They drank a lot and got awfully rowdy. They also traveled a lot.

Stone rose from his chair and walked toward the bar, taking the picture out of his shirt pocket. The cowboys heard him coming and turned around, because everybody on the frontier watched his back all the time. They eyed him suspiciously as he drew closer.

"Howdy," Stone said. "I'm looking for this woman. You ever see her?"

He held out the picture, and one of the cowboys took

it. He was a grizzled young man wearing a black and white checked shirt.

"She's real purty," the cowboy said. He clucked his teeth and showed the picture to the next man. Stone realized they were very drunk. One cowboy looked at the picture and giggled. Two whispered something and another laughed out loud. They passed the picture around, and there were four of them. They smelled like horses, cattle, and too many days on the trail.

The last man was big like Stone. He looked at the picture and winked at the cowboy with the black and white checked shirt. Then he made his face mock solemn and passed the picture back.

"I think I seen the lady," the big cowboy said.

Something in his voice said he was lying, but Stone was hoping that wasn't so. "Where'd you see her?"

The cowboy grinned, showing tobacco-stained teeth. "In a whorehouse in Dodge. She had one guy on top, one guy on the bottom, one guy on each side, and she was doin' it to all of 'em at the same time. I jest took my pecker out and waited my turn with all the other cowboys."

Stone moved to take the photograph out of the cowboy's hand, but the cowboy pulled his hand back.

"What's yer hurry?" the cowboy asked. "I jest wanted to take another look at the whore."

"Give me that picture."

"What's yer rush, boy?"

"I'm not going to tell you again."

"You're not gonna tell me again?" The big cowboy laughed. "What's that supposed to mean?"

Stone hit him with everything he had, and the big cowboy's knees buckled. He went crashing to the floor. Stone turned around and faced the other cowboys.

They glowered at him but not one moved. Stone took the photograph out of the hand of the big cowboy, tucking it into his shirt pocket. The big cowboy was out cold, his lips pulped by the force of the blow. Stone walked back toward the table.

He heard a shuffle of boots behind him, and the cowboys

jumped him before he could turn around. One tackled his waist and another grabbed him around the throat, trying to hold him steady so a third cowboy could punch him in the mouth.

Stone bucked like a wild horse, grabbing the arm of the cowboy who held him by the throat, spinning around. The cowboy's arm bent weirdly, and the cowboy screamed. Stone pushed him out of the way and brought his fist down like a hammer on top of the head of the cowboy who held him around the waist, and the cowboy slid to the floor. The other cowboys charged Stone, and he picked up a table, hurling it at them. They tried to get out of the way, but it crashed into them, knocking them backward.

Stone drew his Colt and pulled back the hammer with his thumb.

"Hold it right there."

They were sprawled all over the floor, their hands hovering above their guns. It was silent for a few seconds as the cowboys stared hatefully at Stone.

One of the cowboys went for his gun, and Stone fired. The other cowboys reached for their guns. Stone rolled out and went into a crouch, fanning the hammer as fast as he could. The saloon filled with gunsmoke, and the bartender dived for cover. Stone dropped to the floor as bullets whizzed over his head. He rolled over and came up on one knee, still firing. Screams filled the air, and bodies went crashing to the floor.

Stone fired his last cartridge, and his hammer went *click*. Gunsmoke was so thick he could barely see. Still on one knee, he thumbed fresh bullets into his Colt. The bartender raised his head.

"It all over?"

Four cowboys lay on the floor; Stone's heart beat wildly. He returned to his table, poured himself a few fingers of whisky, and drank them down.

"Somebody'd better go for the sheriff," the bartender said.

A cowboy put on his hat and ran out of the saloon. Stone took another drink of whisky. All eyes were on him, and he knew he should get out of town, but he had no money, no place to go, and his horse was tired because he'd just arrived. He hoped the sheriff was a reasonable man.

Better stop drinking, he said to himself. He pushed the bottle away and rolled a cigarette. The man with the white mustache approached, carrying his bottle and glass.

"Mighty fine display of shootin' you just put on."

He pulled out a chair and sat at the table opposite Stone. His face was gnarled and weatherbeaten, and his mustache was stained with nicotine.

"My name's Taggart."

"John Stone."

"Live around here?"

"Passing through."

"Where you headed?"

"Looking for somebody." Stone took out the picture of Marie and handed it to him. "Ever see her?"

Taggart looked at the picture. "Who is she?"

"Friend of mine."

"When you get old like me, people start to look alike."

The front door of the saloon opened, and a lanky man with a tin badge on his shirt entered. He took one look around and said: "What the hell happened here!"

Everybody looked at Stone. The sheriff recognized Taggart at the table with Stone.

"Hello there, wagonmaster," the sheriff said. "You didn't kill all these people, did you?"

"This young man did," Taggart replied, "but it was self-defense all the way. I saw the whole thing. They egged him on and shot first."

The sheriff sat at the table and pushed his hat back. He smelled like whisky and gazed longingly at the two bottles on the table.

Taggart shouted, "Bartender—Let's have another glass over here!"

The bartender walked toward the table with a clean glass.

"You see what happened?" the sheriff asked the bartender.

"Yes, sir."

"The wagonmaster here said the cowboys started it."

"That's the way it looked to me, too."

The sheriff turned to Taggart. "Sounds like a simple case of self-defense."

"That's the way it was."

The sheriff reached for the bottle, pouring himself three fingers of whisky. Taggart winked to Stone, who puffed his cigarette calmly, reflecting on frontier justice. You could get off scot-free after shooting people, or a posse could string you up on the spot for stealing a horse, and the little kids would cheer as you swung in the breeze.

The sheriff gulped down his whisky, then took out his notepad. "What's yer name?" he said to Stone.

"John Stone."

"Where you from?"

"Just passing through."

"Where'd you start out from before you was jest passin' through?"

"South Carolina."

"You say these men egged you on?"

"That's right."

"And you shot *all* of them?"

"Yes."

"Must be awful fast. Where'd you learn to shoot like that?"

Stone was silent.

"I said, where'd you learn to shoot like that?"

"In the war."

"You fought for Bobby Lee, I take it."

"That's right."

The sheriff held out his hand and smiled. "So did I."

They shook hands. The sheriff put on his hat and walked toward the bar, where he conferred with the bartender, who poured him another drink. Taggart puffed his cigar and looked at John Stone.

"What did you do in the war?"

"I was in the cavalry."

"What rank?"

"What does it matter?"

"I'm lookin' for a good man."

"To do what?"

"Scout, for my wagon train. Interested?"

"Maybe."

"What was your rank?"

"Captain."

"Line or staff?"

"Line."

"Want the job?"

"I don't know anything about wagon trains."

"If you could command cavalry in war, you can work a wagon train."

"How many wagons?"

"Maybe a dozen."

"What's the destination?"

"Texas."

"That's a long trip," Stone said.

"That's why we need a good scout."

"Should be a lot of good men around."

"That's what you think."

The sheriff walked toward them from the bar. "Everybody backed yer story," he said to Stone. "Yer free to leave."

Stone took the picture out of his shirt pocket. "Ever see this woman, Sheriff?"

The sheriff looked at it. "Don't think so. Them cowboys you shot got friends. I'd be on my guard if'n I was you."

Stone put the picture back into his shirt pocket, and the sheriff walked toward the bar. Taggart leaned toward Stone.

"Lots of people go to Texas," Taggart said. "Yer lady friend in the picture might be there."

Stone drained his glass.

"Have another drink."

"Can't afford to drink any more."

"I'm buyin'."

Stone filled his glass to the halfway mark, then rolled another cigarette.

"In other words, you're broke," Taggart said.

"Damn near."

"What were you plannin' to do for money?"

"Don't know yet."

"You might as well take me up on my offer. You got nothin' else to do."

"Texas is a long way off."

"Only a month or two, dependin' on conditions."

"We haven't talked money yet."

Taggart held up his hand. "Can't pay much. It's a poor-ass wagon train. Mostly dirt farmers and church folk."

"How much?"

"We'll supply your meals, shelter and horses."

"How much?"

"Thirty dollars a month."

Stone sipped his whisky. Thirty dollars a month was what cowboys earned, but he was down to his last few dollars and had no hot prospects. And maybe Taggart was right—maybe Marie was in Texas.

"Let me think about it."

The door to the saloon opened, and men wearing ponchos entered. They lifted the dead bodies and carried them out into the storm. The bartender dropped sawdust on the blood and moved the tables back to where they'd been before the gunplay.

Taggart took out a cigar. "You hungry?"

"Yes."

Taggart raised his hand in the air. "Bartender—two steak dinners with all the trimmin's."

The bartender walked through a doorway into a back room. Lightning flashed in the street outside, and thunder shook the rafters of the saloon.

"When's your wagon train leaving?" Stone asked Taggart.

"Few days from now."

"Expect Indian trouble?"

"Sometimes we run into 'em and sometimes we don't.

If yer worried about Indians, you might as well hightail it back to South Carolina. There's Indians all over the frontier. You can't git away from 'em."

"What happens if you're attacked by Indians?"

"What you *think* happens?"

"Is it common?"

"What do you call common?"

"Is every wagon train attacked?"

"Not every one, but sometimes a wagon train might get hit two or three times. Sometimes we have trouble with outlaw gangs, too. A wagon train ain't no picnic. If yer worried about fightin', maybe this ain't the job for you. You got a family?"

"Not any more."

"You sound like the kind of person who might've been well-off before the war."

"Don't want to talk about it."

"Got something to hide?"

"Don't like to dredge up the past."

Taggart smiled. "Just a curious old man, that's all. Don't take no offense. Can't help bein' curious about a man who just shot four cowboys like they was nothin'."

"I was lucky."

"People make their own luck. You knew what you were doin'. Moved like a cat. Yer a real fighter. I know somethin' about fightin' because I was in the war myself. We wasn't on the same side, and I weren't no officer—I was a sergeant in the infantry. I might've taken a shot at you on one of those days, or you might've taken a shot at me, but here we are in this saloon together, and we're goin' to Texas together."

"Who said I'm going to Texas?"

"You got no job and no money. What else you got to do?"

Taggart poured whisky into Stone's glass, and the bartender placed a steak platter in front of Stone. The aroma rose to his nostrils, and he picked up his knife and fork, cutting into the steak. He didn't know if it was the whisky or not, but he was warming up to the old wagonmaster.

Taggart washed down his food with whisky. "That gal in the picture—what's she to you?"

"We were engaged."

"What happened to her?"

"That's what I'm trying to figure out."

"How long you been lookin' for her?"

"Since the war."

"What if you don't find her?"

"I'll find her."

"Maybe you should go back home and put yer life back together."

"Don't have anything to put together."

"The gal was engaged to you, and she just upped and ran away?"

"When I returned home after the war, she was gone. Some folks said she went west with a Union officer, but I can't imagine her going anywhere with a Union officer. All I know is I'm looking for her."

"What happened to yer family?"

"All dead."

"You must love her an awful lot to be huntin' her this way. Where'd you meet her?"

"We were neighbors, grew up together."

"Come on to Texas with me. Start a new life. Maybe the gal's there and maybe she ain't, but you'll never know if you don't go and see for yerself."

"Where you from, Taggart?"

"I'm like horseshit. I been all over the road."

"I'll need an advance on my wages."

"What for?"

"Another Colt."

"What's the matter with the one you got?"

"Might need six extra shots someday."

The door to the saloon was thrown open, and a group of hard-looking men stepped inside. Their leader wore a black leather frock coat, and he hollared: "Who shot my cowboys!"

The saloon fell silent. Everyone looked at Stone. The man in the black leather coat stomped across the saloon, pushing tables and chairs out of his way. Stone got to his feet, and Taggart rose beside him.

"This isn't your fight," Stone said.

"It ain't so easy to find a good scout these days."

The man in the black leather coat was followed by eight cowboys, and all of them stopped in front of Stone and Taggart.

"You shot my cowboys?" the man asked, looking back and forth between Stone and Taggart.

"I did," Stone said.

The man looked at Taggart. "How about you?"

"I saw everything, and it was self-defense all the way."

"It was," the bartender agreed. "I saw it, too."

"Ain't the way I heard it," the man said, measuring Stone. "You done messed with the wrong people, boy."

He and his men stepped away, except for one cowboy facing Stone in a gunfighter's stance, legs spread apart, right hand dangling in the air.

"You might be big," the cowboy said, "but you ain't bigger than a bullet."

The bartender held out his hand. "Now wait a minute! We don't want no more shootin' in here!"

The cowboy wore two guns in crisscrossed holsters tied down and had long bowed legs. A rattlesnake skin was his hatband, and evidently he was the fastest gun they had.

"You killed some friends of mine," the cowboy said, wiggling his fingers. "I like to know the name of the man I shoot. What's yours?"

"Make your move."

Stone stood tense and ready, and that old, wild, war feeling came over him. The cowboy narrowed his eyes. His hand was poised in the air above his gun. Suddenly his hand dropped down.

Stone's long fingers slapped the handle of his gun and brought the weapon up fast. He pulled the trigger, and the saloon resounded with his gunshot.

The tip of the cowboy's gun barrel still was in his holster when the bullet slammed into him. He took a step backward and stared at Stone in disbelief. Stone fired again, and the cowboy spun around, dropping his gun. He fell to the floor.

"Who's next?" Stone asked. He pointed his gun at the man in the black leather coat. "How about you?"

Raw animal hatred was in the man's eyes, but he didn't move.

"Go ahead," Stone said. "The world can do without another lowdown coyote."

The man held his hands steady where Stone could see them. Stone swept his gun back and forth over the other cowboys.

"Anybody else feel froggy?"

They made no effort to reach for their guns.

"Get out of here," Stone said, "and take your friend with you."

Two of the cowboys picked up the one Stone had shot and carried him toward the door. The others followed, and the man in the long black leather coat said evenly to Stone, "Hope we meet again someday."

"If we do, I'm going to kill you."

The man in the black leather coat turned around and pushed his way through his cowboys. He headed toward the door, and his cowboys followed him. Pausing at the door, he aimed one last malevolent glance over his shoulder at Stone, then pushed the doors open and stepped outside.

"What's his name?" Stone asked.

"Dillon," replied the bartender. "He's the ramrod of the Rafter K."

Stone sat and reloaded his Colt. "I've got to get another one of these . . . could use six extra bullets."

Taggart sat opposite him. "Yer a crazy son of a bitch. Just went up against nine men and didn't flinch. Don't care about yer life much, looks like."

Stone reached for the bottle and filled his glass to the brim, then raised it to his lips, spilling a few drops on the table.

"You better watch out for them cowboys," Taggart said. "They'll be gunnin' for you."

"That's why I want another Colt." Stone picked up his knife and fork and resumed eating.

"Maybe we'd better get out of town."

"I'm not finished."

"Yer liable to be finished more than you want if they come back."

"They know some of them will die if they draw on me, and nobody wants to die."

They had apple pie for dessert and drank coffee. Taggart smoked a cigar and Stone rolled a cigarette. The composition of the saloon changed as men staggered drunkenly out the door, and new arrivals walked forthrightly toward the bar. Some men pointed at Stone. He hoped there weren't any crazy young kids who wanted to make their reputations by shooting him in the back.

Taggart examined Stone's worn clothing, stubbled cheeks, firm jaw. He looked tired, and there was deep sorrow in his eyes.

"You'll like Texas," he said. "You might decide to stay there. It's practically a whole nation all to itself, with plenty of land for everybody. If you ain't seen it, you can't imagine it. It's a whole new world."

"What will my duties be as your scout?"

"You'll ride ahead of the wagon train and report what's there. You'll look for water and good campsites. If you see Injuns, you'll come back and tell us. Where'd you plan to stay tonight?"

"I'd planned to make camp outside town."

"I got my set-up out on the prairie. You can spend the night in my wagon now that yer on the payroll. We'll pick up some supplies and leave."

They walked to the counter, and Taggart bought canned food and bacon, stuffing the goods into burlap bags. They put on their ponchos and headed toward the door.

The rain came down ferociously. They ran across the street to the stable and saddled their horses. Then they rode out into the rain that fell in a roar.

The boardwalk was deserted, and lanterns were visible behind windows. The middle of the street was a morass, its surface pelted by driving rain. The horses walked through it, feeling cold water roll down their flanks. Stone hunched underneath his poncho, his hat low over his eyes, water pouring off the brim.

The road became a trail that meandered over the rolling prairie. Lightning made jagged white lines against the dark gray clouds. Stone felt a chill underneath his poncho.

During the war, he'd lived outdoors for most of five years, often eating in the rain, sleeping in it, and fighting in it.

There was nothing more difficult than hand-to-hand combat in a downpour. You couldn't get a foothold or handhold because everything was slimy with blood and muck. You rolled around in it and tried to kill your man.

A knobby old tree emerged out of the mists.

"We turn off here," Taggart said.

The horses trudged onto the new trail, and the rain fell so heavily Stone could see only twenty or thirty feet in the distance. Beyond that was a gray wall.

I'm going to Texas. He'd intended to move west more slowly, but the wagon train was free, and he'd even get paid and get his grub, too. There was only one catch: the Indians.

Since coming to the frontier, he'd heard lots about Indians. They killed white people whenever they could, and the wagon train would pass through the middle of the most hazardous Indian country in America.

Taggart's covered wagon was nestled in the hills, and his horses were gathered under a canvas roof that spilled rainwater down its sides. Taggart and Stone unsaddled their riding horses and hitched them under the canvas with the team horses, then climbed into the back of the wagon.

It was a small space, and Taggart lit the kerosene lantern, turning up the wick. His lined face glowed orange as he plunged another cigar into his mouth and lit it from the flame in the lantern.

"When'll the others get here?" Stone asked.

"The first should start showin' up day after tomorrow. The others'll straggle in durin' the rest of the week. I 'spect we'll leave Monday. There's one more thing I forgot to tell you. *Leave the womenfolk alone.* I don't want any fightin' over womenfolk."

"I'm engaged to get married," Stone said. "I won't bother the women."

"When you see Alice McGhee, yer liable to forget yer engaged. Sometimes a pretty woman can cause more trouble on a wagon train than a Comanche war party. The men fight over her, and then the other women fight with her, and it's a mess." Taggart puffed his cigar. "Gittin' late. Gonna turn in."

Taggart arranged his bed, consisting of blankets on the floorboards of the wagon, then stuck his cigar butt outside and let the rain put it out. He dropped the cigar into his hat and stretched out on his blankets.

"Night," he said.

Stone smoked his cigarette in the darkness and listened to the rain pounding on the canvas. He thought of corpses in puddles and tiny rivers of blood flowing in all directions. The stench had been the worst. It could stop a man in his tracks. Your skin got white and shrivelled, and your feet went numb. Your ammunition wouldn't fire. The men were sick. War in the rain had been a nightmare. He shivered as he pulled his blanket over his shoulders and rested his head on his saddle. The thunder in the distance sounded like cannon.

He was going to Texas with an old wagonmaster who'd fought against him in the war. Funny how everything turned over onto itself. He closed his eyes and listened to the rain. Gradually he sank into slumber and dreamed of cavalry advancing to the front through the rain.

2

HE WAS AWAKENED by the smell of coffee and bacon. Poking his head outside the canvas, he saw Taggart preparing breakfast in front of a fire.

"Stick yer head in the feed bag," Taggart said.

The rain had stopped, but the sky was full of clouds. Stone pulled on his boots and climbed down from the wagon. He sat next to Taggart and gazed across the clearing at a big black bird perched high in the branches of a tree.

This was the time of day Stone liked best. The world had just been born anew, and anything was possible.

Taggart handed him a tin plate filled with bacon and beans and covered with two sourdough biscuits. "Need to get supplies in town today. You don't have to come in if you don't want to."

"Want to buy another gun, so I'll be going in, too."

"There might be gunplay."

"If you're worried about getting shot, I'll go in alone."

"Rambunctious, ain't you? Just remember there's always somebody faster."

"Can't hide my head under my pillow because somebody's faster."

"We'll go in together. Watch each other's back."

"It's not you they're mad at."

Taggart lowered his voice an octave. "Like I said, we'll watch each other's back."

Stone ate his beans. A squirrel ran across the clearing, paused to look at them, and continued on its way.

"You a gunfighter?" Taggart asked.

"No."

"You talk like one. Hope you don't die like one."

After breakfast they hitched the horses to the wagon and rode to town. The trail was deserted, and a mist hung over the prairie. Taggart sat upright on his seat, smoking a cigar.

"If we see Rafter K horses, it might not be a good idea to spend much time in town."

"They won't stop me from doing what I want."

"You lookin' to die?"

"I'm buying another gun."

"Yer gonna need one, crazy as you are."

The main street of Crawford was crowded with riders and wagons. Stone spotted a sign that said GUNSMITH, and Taggart angled the horses toward it as a bullwhacker with a load of buffalo hides passed on the other side of the street.

Taggart stopped the wagon in front of the gunsmith's shop, and Stone jumped to the ground. He stepped onto the boardwalk and turned around quickly. Two dirty-faced boys ran by, followed by a lady in calico. Taggart joined Stone on the sidewalk.

"Don't see any Rafter K brands."

Stone entered the gunsmith's shop and saw pistols in the display cases and rifles mounted on the walls with the heads of an antelope, buffalo, and mountain goat. A man with a stringy black mustache sat behind the counter reading an old newspaper.

"What can I do fer you?"

"I want to buy a used Colt to match this one." Stone laid his gun on the counter.

The man looked at it, then took a similar one out of the display case and handed it to him. Stone felt its weight, cocked the hammer, aimed down the barrel, and pulled the trigger. It felt the same as the Colt he had.

"Take it out back and fire a few cartridges if you want."

Stone walked down the passageway and came to the yard. Before him were bottles and cans on a plank suspended between two barrels. Stone thumbed six cartridges into the Colt, raised it, and took aim. He fired all six shots in rapid succession, and six cans went flying into the air.

He returned to the gunsmith's shop. "I'll need another belt and holster."

The gunsmith rummaged through a box and came up with two identical belts and holsters. "If yer gonna carry two guns, yer holsters should be matched. I'll take the one yer wearin' in trade."

Stone pulled off his holster and strapped on the two the man had brought him. He crisscrossed them and slung them low, tying them to his legs. Then he quick-drew both a few times.

"How much?"

"Twelve dollars."

Taggart stepped forward and paid the gunsmith. Stone holstered the guns and walked toward the door, aware of the new weight on his body. He stepped onto the boardwalk and looked down the street to the saloon where he'd shot those men yesterday.

Taggart joined him on the boardwalk. "Let's go to the store."

"Why don't we have a drink first?"

"Are you crazy?"

"When a man first comes to town, he usually stops off at a drinking establishment. It's the civilized thing to do."

"If you git killed, how'm I gonna git my twelve dollars back?"

"Take my horse and guns."

Stone walked toward the saloon, spurs jangling and the butts of his guns hanging wide. Taggart caught up with him.

"I think there's somethin' wrong with yer mind. You

must be lookin' to die. If there's boys from the Rafter K in there, they'll shoot you like a dog."

"Man's got a right to have a drink if he wants one."

"Yer a stubborn son of a bitch!"

They passed the sheriff's office, a barber shop, and a lawyer's office. The sun had come out, and steam rose from puddles of water in the street. Then they came to the saloon. They looked at the horses tied to the rail, and some of them carried the Rafter K brand.

"You don't have to come in," Stone said to Taggart.

"You go in that saloon, and they'll carry you out feet first."

Stone moved toward the swinging doors. Taggart grabbed his arm.

"Why?" Taggart asked.

"I want a drink."

"You can get a drink someplace else."

"I want one here."

Stone shook loose and stepped through the swinging doors. The bar was to the left; men drank and talked loudly. Stone spotted Dillon, the ramrod of the Rafter K, wearing his black leather coat, one foot on the bar rail.

Dillon looked up from his glass and saw Stone advancing. Their eyes met, and Stone walked past him toward an opening at the bar. He placed his foot on the rail and waited for the bartender to take his order.

It was the same bartender who'd been on duty yesterday, and his hand trembled so much he could barely pour whisky into the glass of the cowboy in front of him. Taggart took his place beside Stone, and everything became quiet.

The bartender walked fearfully toward Stone.

"Two whiskies," Stone said.

The bartender placed two glasses and a bottle on the bar, then stepped back out of the way. Stone poured whisky into his glass and passed the bottle to Taggart.

Somebody spoke at the end of the bar: "Son of a bitch got a lot of nerve walkin' in here like that."

Stone sipped the whisky, rinsing his mouth with the fiery liquid. He looked relaxed but was ready to draw and fire.

"I say we should kill him where he stands," the voice said.

Stone looked down the bar in the direction of the voice. "Why don't you try it?"

There was silence for a few moments, then the cowboy pushed himself away from the bar and walked toward Stone, stopping ten feet in front of him. The cowboy wore one gun in a holster tied to his leg and a bear's tooth on a thong around his neck. His hat was low over his eyes.

Everyone got out of the way. Stone stepped away from the bar and faced the cowboy.

"How many of you idiots from the Rafter K do I have to kill?"

"Yer killin' days are over."

They faced each other. The bartender raised his eyes above the bar, took one look, and ducked again.

Dillon spoke: "Finish him off, Tandy."

Tandy was shorter than Stone, with a shadowy growth of beard on his jowls. He spread his legs apart and poised his hand above his gun, gazing at Stone through flinty eyes. He looked like a coiled spring.

Tandy's hand dove toward his gun, but Stone's two Colts already were clearing their holsters, and he pulled the triggers. The guns fired simultaneously and Tandy looked like he'd been struck in the chest by a tree. He staggered backward, an expression of astonishment on his face.

The gun fell out of his hand, and the air was thick with gunsmoke. Tandy's eyes glazed over, and his body undulated, then he went crashing to the floor.

The death energy hit Stone, that wild spiral of a man's spirit leaving. It bolted through his body and left him cold. He looked at the men from the Rafter K, smoke rising from both barrels of his Colts.

"Who's next?"

Nobody said anything. The saloon had become silent, and everyone stood still as a statue. Stone stared at the cowboys from the Rafter K while the pool of blood widened around Tandy.

Taggart stood near Stone, facing the cowboys from the Rafter K, his hand above his Remington. The men from the Rafter K knew they could win in the end, but the price would be high. Nobody made a move.

Stone walked toward Dillon, his Colts still leveled. Dillon stood in front of the bar, the handle of his gun showing through the opening in his black leather coat. He made no attempt to go for it.

Stone stopped in front of him.

"You must be a real bad hombre to be ramrod of the Rafter K."

Dillon didn't say a word. The barrels of Stone's Colts were inches from his chest.

"I'll give you a fair chance," Stone said.

He took three steps backward and dropped his Colts into their holsters. Then he spread his legs. "Make your move."

Dillon tried to keep his fear hidden, but it was visible in the pallor on his face and in his thinned lips.

"I'm waiting," Stone said.

The ramrod of the Rafter K was being humiliated in front of his men. Dillon looked as though he were going to faint.

Stone stared at Dillon. "You look to be the kind of scum who'd shoot a man in the back, so here's my back. Go ahead and take a shot—if you've got the grit."

Stone turned around slowly, presenting his back to Dillon, and if he heard the faintest hostile sound, he'd hit the floor and pull his Colts, but nothing happened. They were afraid of him. He'd backed them down.

"Guess I've got no takers," Stone said. He stepped toward the bar. "Bartender—can I get a glass of whisky?"

The bartender raised his head, reached for the bottle, and poured the drink. Taggart joined Stone at the bar. Men from the Rafter K picked up Tandy and carried him out the door, followed by all the cowboys who rode for that brand; including Dillon.

The bartender picked up his bucket of sawdust and carried it around the bar, dropping handfuls on the blood. Stone sipped his whisky, feeling light-headed and strange. Adrenaline rushed through his arteries, and he felt as if he could run all the way to Texas.

Taggart turned and looked at Stone. "Yer even crazier than I thought."

Stone reached for his bag of tobacco. His hands trembled and his mouth was dry as he rolled the cigarette. He'd won, but it could've gone the other way.

"If you ever see a Rafter K brand again, you'd better run for yer life," Taggart said. "Next time they'll shoot you on sight."

Stone lit his cigarette. The doors opened and the sheriff entered the saloon followed by one of his deputies.

"Now what the hell happened in here?" the sheriff said.

"Another cowboy from the Rafter K got shot," the bartender replied and pointed his thumb at Stone. "It was him again."

The sheriff looked down the bar at Stone sipping his whisky. "I guess it was self-defense?"

"That's right."

"How'd it happen?" the sheriff asked the bartender.

"The cowboy from the Rafter K braced this man here, and this man beat him to the draw."

"I'm a witness," Taggart said. "That's the way it was."

The sheriff pushed back the brim of his hat and moved toward the bar. "Whisky."

The bartender filled a glass; the sheriff raised it to his lips and knocked it back. Then he looked at Stone.

"If I was you, I'd leave town."

"I am leaving town—in a few days."

Stone filled his glass with whisky. He hated fear and took the offensive whenever it came. It was the only way to deal with fear.

Taggart finished his glass. "We'd better git rollin' along. Got a lot to do."

Stone downed his whisky, readjusted the cavalry hat on

his head, and headed for the door, stepping over the puddle of blood in the middle of the floor.

A crowd had gathered across the street, looking at the saloon. Taggart stepped through the swinging doors and joined Stone.

"Let's go to the store."

They walked side by side down the planked sidewalk. A few kids ran beside them in the street, staring at them in awe. A drunk lay sprawled on a bench in front of the undertaker's office, and they stepped over his legs. Finally they came to the store.

It was dark and cavernous, with goods piled everywhere. A group of men sat around a long low table.

"What can I do for you?" asked the bald man behind the counter.

Taggart took a list out of his shirt pocket and laid it on the counter. Stone sat on a chair in the corner and smoked his cigarette.

Beside him was a stack of hides that smelled like new leather. It was quiet in the store, and the bald man placed a crate of beans on the counter. Taggart was buying his main supplies for the trip to Texas, and Stone thought of the fight in the saloon. It wasn't the first time he'd been braced by a stranger. Frontier saloons were full of men who wanted to play with guns.

"I'll get the wagon," Taggart said.

"I'll go with you."

"Stay here and watch the grub."

Taggart walked out of the store. Stone wondered if the cowboys from the Rafter K would try to dry gulch him. He rose and stood in the doorway, watching Taggart head toward the wagon.

The street was crowded with riders and buggies. Stone looked at the windows and roofs across the street but didn't see anything suspicious. He didn't think the cowboys from the Rafter K would take the chance of shooting innocent people, but later, on the trail, there might be trouble.

Stone looked at Taggart climbing into the wagon. The

old man had stood beside him in a fight where he might be killed, but he never hesitated.

Taggart stopped the wagon in front of the store. He and Stone loaded the supplies in back, then picked up the tailgate and fastened it. They climbed onto the wagon, and Stone scanned the rooftops. Taggart flicked the reins, and the horses walked into the street.

They rode out of town, and Stone held his rifle in his hands, peering into alleys and looking through open windows for the gleam of gun barrels. They came to the edge of town, and ahead was the open prairie.

"Thanks for standin' with me back there," Stone said.

Taggart lit a cigar. "I don't know whether yer a brave man or a damn fool."

Crawford receded in the distance behind them. Stone's eyes roved back and forth on the prairie, wondering if the cowboys from the Rafter K were out there someplace, waiting for them.

"You must've been hell in the war," Taggart said. "I'm shore glad yer on my side now. When you showed yer back to Dillon, I thought you was a dead man. Someday yer going to try that with the wrong person, and that'll be the last time you try it."

They returned to camp without incident, unhitched the horses, and set them out to graze. Taggart heated beans and flavored them with his special spices, then served them with thick wedges of tinned meat.

They sat by the fire. The sun was overhead, and only a few wispy clouds were in the sky.

"Yer the fastest man I ever seen," Taggart said. "Can't forget how you stood up to 'em. Why'd you taunt 'em?"

Stone shrugged.

"Life is cheap when yer young. When yer older, it's more dear."

"Why did you stand with me?"

"A good scout is hard to find."

"I don't know anything about being a scout."

"I can always use a man with a gun. You got just the kind of experience I'm lookin' for, and what you don't know you can learn, but I think you might be in for some disappointment down the line. What if you don't find that gal of yer'n, or what if she's married to somebody else when you do find her? Then what'll you do?"

"I don't know."

"You'd better think about it. Every soldier's got to figure out his line of retreat just in case." Taggart raised his arm and swept it over the horizon. "You like this country?"

"It's beautiful."

"You oughta think about settlin' down out here."

"I do think about it."

"Let me give you some advice. I know you believe yer woman is the only woman in the world, but I've been around a lot longer than you, and I know better. All wimmin are pretty much alike, when you get down to it. All you need to do is find a good one, and there's lots of good ones out here, wimmin who ain't afraid to work, wimmin with grit. If I was you, I'd pick one and settle down while yer still young. Yer liable never to find that one yer lookin' for, and you'll throw yer whole damn life away."

"Maybe I'll give up someday," Stone said, "but not yet. Got to keep looking. A person doesn't vanish off the face of the earth."

3

THE FIRST WAGON arrived the next morning. It contained
a family of farmers from Pennsylvania. Old Stewart Donahue had a white beard and wore suspenders. His wife,
Martha, was stout and always busy. They had two big
strapping teen-aged boys and one girl nine years old, a
pretty, shy, little thing who liked to pick flowers on the
prairie.

The next wagon had three miners aboard, burly men in
dirty shirts and canvas pants, all wearing beards. They had
gold dust in their eyes, and their names were Wayne Collins, Joe Doakes, and Georgie Saulnier.

Then came the preacher man, the Reverend Joshua
McGhee, his wife, Doris, and his daughter, Alice, the one
Taggart had said was so beautiful, and he hadn't lied. She
was a redhead with the face of an angel.

"Glad you could make it," Taggart said to McGhee,
shaking his hand. "This is our scout, John Stone."

Stone shook hands with Reverend McGhee. He figured
Alice was no more than nineteen. Her eyes sparkled with
delight as she looked around the prairie.

"It's so beautiful here!"

"Watch out for Injuns," Taggart said.

Reverend McGhee looked at Stone. "I take it you've
made this passage before."

Stone was about to say that he was new to the territory, but Taggart interrupted him. "Captain Stone has made the trip many times. He's a former cavalry officer."

"Where do you want me to set up?" Reverend McGhee asked.

"Anywhere that's convenient for you. The stream's that-away, and there's plenny of good grazing around here as you can see."

The Reverend McGhee slapped his reins against the haunches of his horses, and the horses pulled the wagon away. When it was out of earshot, Stone turned to Taggart.

"Why'd you tell him I'm an experienced scout?"

"What he don't know won't hurt him."

Taggart winked and walked away. Stone looked at the McGhee wagon. It had stopped, and Alice was climbing down from her seat. She turned and looked at him, and he looked back. Their eyes met, and Stone turned away.

Just before lunch, the Fenwicks arrived, another farm family. They had the newest wagon and wore new clothes. Jason and Mary Fenwick were in their early thirties and had four young children, two boys and two girls. Taggart welcomed them to the wagon train and introduced them to Stone.

"Our scout," Taggart said, slapping Stone on the back.

"Pleased to meet you," Jason Fenwick said.

Stone liked the look of Fenwick. They shook hands, and then the Fenwicks moved toward their camping spot.

"Nice family," Taggart said. "Too bad if the Comanches get 'em."

In the early afternoon, a rickety old wagon pulled into the clearing. It swayed from side to side and looked as though it might tip over. Three women were perched on the front seat. The one with the reins was middle-aged and plump, with a red bandana on her head. The other two were young and pretty.

"Howdy, Mister Taggart!" shouted the woman in the middle. "Waal, we made it!"

"Glad to see you," Taggart said. "Let me introduce

my scout, Captain John Stone. Captain Stone—Miss Bottom."

Stone tipped his hat. "How do you do, Miss Bottom."

"Not too bad, Captain Stone. This here's Miss Daisy Sommers, and this is Miss Shirley Clanton."

Miss Bottom fluttered her eyelashes. Misses Sommers and Clanton looked Stone up and down with more than routine interest, while he wondered what three women were doing traveling across the open plains without a man.

The wagon moved off, and Stone turned to Taggart. "What the hell was *that* all about?" he asked.

"What do you think it's all about?"

"They sure as hell don't look like farmers."

"They're dance hall girls. You know what I'm talkin' about. Texas needs wimmin, otherwise the cowboys'll be screwin' their horses after a while."

The lonely plain became transformed into a scene of domesticity. Women washed clothes and prepared meals, while men watered horses, chopped wood, and fixed whatever was wrong with their wagons. Children played hide and seek in the tall grass. Toward suppertime another wagon arrived, this one containing two dudes, one wearing a derby and the other a stovetop hat.

Taggart and Stone walked toward the wagon. The dudes wore striped shirts with suspenders, the top buttons of their shirts unfastened. The one on the left was stout, and the one on the right, holding the reins, was slim. Their faces were sunburned, as if they'd only recently come into the sunlight.

Taggart introduced himself and Stone. The men said they were Tad Holton and Sam Drake.

"When'll we be pullin' out?" asked Drake, the one who held the reins.

"Soon as the other wagons get here."

Drake leaned forward and grinned like a hyena. "Think we might find a good card game in that town we just passed?"

"There's some wild cowboys in that town."

"We can take care of ourselves. Nice meeting you, Captain Stone."

Drake slapped the reins, and the wagon pulled away. Taggart turned to Stone. "Wouldn't get drawn into any games with 'em, if I was you."

"Looks like we've got a little bit of everything here."

"That's what a wagon train is—a little bit of everything."

Fires were lit around the campsite, and the sun sank toward the horizon. After supper, Stone checked his horse, a sorrel with three white boots. He'd bought the horse a month ago in Ohio from a horse breeder who'd fought for Nathan Bedford Forrest.

Stone walked back to the wagon he shared with Taggart and sat against one of the wheels. He rolled a cigarette and placed it between his lips. Raucous sounds came to him from across the way. It sounded as if the miners had whisky.

Taggart was nearby, sitting next to the fire, gazing at the glowing embers. Stone could see that the old wagon-master was lost in thought. He heard a shriek of laughter on the other side of the campsite; it sounded like the dance hall girls. The campsite was getting lively.

Stone gazed up at the stars. When he'd been in the cavalry, he'd often used the stars as guides, like a compass. The North Star was the most important one, and they'd leave in a few days in the opposite direction, toward Texas.

He heard the approach of footsteps, and it was the Reverend Joshua McGhee. "Mister Taggart—can't you do something about the noise? My family and I'd like to turn in early, but we can't sleep with all that ruckus. Sounds like somebody's got some whisky and having themselves an *orgy*."

"I doubt if it's that serious, Reverend."

"Well, that's what it sounds like. Satan does his best work at night. I think you should go over there and settle those folks down."

"I'll look into it," Taggart said.

Reverend McGhee walked away. Taggart waited until

he was out of earshot. "Pain in the ass," Taggart muttered. "Let's go talk to them miners."

Stone and Taggart walked across the campsite. Stone was a head taller than Taggart and wider in the shoulders. Stone looked hard as a rock whereas Taggart was getting soft.

They drew closer to the miners' wagon. A kerosene lamp shone inside, casting shadows against the canvas walls. The rear of the wagon was covered with a canvas curtain. One of the miners whooped inside, and a woman giggled.

"Hello there!" said Taggart.

Suddenly it became silent inside the wagon. Then the head of Wayne Collins, one of the miners, poked itself outside. Collins was moon-faced and grizzled. "Whataya want?"

"Think you can keep it down in there? We've had some complaints."

"Who made the complaints?"

"Never mind. Just keep it down. We got people here who're tryin' to sleep."

Suddenly the canvas curtain was pulled to the side, revealing the interior of the wagon. The three dance hall girls were seated with the miners, and all were disheveled and bleary-eyed. The miner called Joe Doakes had pulled the curtain aside, and he didn't look happy.

"What the hell's the problem out here!" he demanded.

"I'm askin' you to be quiet in there," Taggart replied.

"What the hell do I have to be quiet for?"

"Yer botherin' other people."

"To hell with 'em!" He held a bottle of whisky in the air. "Come on in and have a drink!"

Stone stepped forward. "The wagonmaster asked you to be quiet. I think you'd better do it."

"Nobody tells me what to do!"

Stone rushed toward the wagon, grabbed Doakes by the front of his shirt, and pulled him down to the ground. It happened so quickly that Doakes didn't know what hit him. "Huh?" he said. "What?"

Stone held Doakes' shirt in both his fists and looked down at him. "You're going to be quiet, all right?"

"I hear ya," Doakes said weakly.

Stone picked him up as if he were light as a feather and put him back in the wagon. Then he said goodnight and walked away. Taggart followed him.

"Thanks for yer help," Taggart said.

"I think I'm gonna turn in."

Stone walked to the stream. He washed his face and hands in the stream and rinsed out his mouth with the cool sweet water. Then he turned around and walked back to the campsite on the narrow trail.

He saw a figure ahead of him on the trail. It was a woman, wearing a long dress. They approached each other, and Stone saw Alice McGhee, daughter of the preacher man.

He touched his finger to the brim of his hat. "Evening."

She looked up into his eyes, and her face glowed in the moonlight. "Thank you very much for quieting those rowdy people down. It was very brave and good of you."

"You're welcome."

"Where are you from?"

"South Carolina."

"We're from Michigan. Mister Taggart said you were in the war."

"Yes, ma'am."

"We feel very safe, being here with you, Captain Stone. What do you plan to do when you get to Texas?"

"Don't know."

"If you needed a job, I'm sure my father could find something for you on our farm. We're buying a farm in Texas, you know."

"I'll keep it in mind."

"Why are you going to Texas, Captain Stone?"

Stone took out the picture and showed it to her. "Ever see her?"

Alice held the picture up in the moonlight. "Don't believe I have. Who is she?"

"Friend of mine."

"Are you in love with her?"

"Yes, ma'am."

"She's a lucky girl. Hope you find her someday."

Alice handed the picture back, and Stone placed it in his shirt pocket. They looked at each other awkwardly for a few moments, then she smiled and continued on her way to the stream.

Stone made his way back to Taggart's wagon and arranged his blanket and saddle near the faint glowing embers of the fire. He lay down and covered himself with the blanket, rolling over onto his side, thinking about Alice McGhee. She was all sweetness and purity, with an expression so innocent it made a man afraid of saying the wrong thing.

Stone felt attracted to Alice McGhee. It wasn't often that a man saw a truly beautiful woman on the frontier. Somehow the frontier grinded women down and made them old before their time. Then Stone thought of Marie, and a deep longing came over him. Alice McGhee was pretty, but Marie Higgins owned his soul.

He felt pain underneath his hip. A small pebble was there, digging into his skin. He reached for it and threw it away then rolled onto his back.

Above him were the blazing heavens. Stone stared at vast galaxies and the mountains of the moon. Before the war, he'd had a huge bedroom all to himself on his father's plantation, Albemarle. He'd had his own personal servant who did whatever he asked, and he'd never done a lick of work until he went to West Point. Now he was sleeping on the ground underneath the stars, in dirty clothes, with a pittance in his pocket. He'd fallen to the bottom, another rat scurrying around the frontier, trying to survive.

He closed his eyes and drifted away into the vast black night.

4

MORE WAGONS ARRIVED during the next two days, carrying farmers, dudes from the East, Irish immigrants, rowdies, adventurers, gold prospectors, businessmen, and just plain riff-raff.

The encampment swelled in size and became a small town. Some people became friends and others became enemies, just as in any small town. Taggart was the mayor, and Stone became the police force. An atmosphere of excitement and adventure filled the air. Soon they'd be crossing the great plains, following their destinies, and every one of them hoped to become rich in Texas.

On Sunday morning, the Reverend Joshua McGhee held an open-air prayer service in which he asked God to bless the journey. About three-quarters of the people attended, and Stone was there, sitting in back, because he was a God-fearing man.

Doris McGhee, wife of the reverend, had assembled a choir, and they sang "Rock of Ages" at the termination of the service. Young Alice was in the choir, and Stone couldn't keep his eyes off her.

Most spent the rest of the day preparing for the trip, except for the gamblers and a few others who went into town. Stone studied the maps Taggart provided him. Taggart had made the trip numerous times and marked the route with a pen, indicating where water could be found. They hoped to cover a specific distance every day, which would vary according to the terrain.

Stone rolled a cigarette and sat on the ground looking around the campsite. He'd been sizing up the various travelers ever since they arrived so he'd know what to expect from each of them.

The farmers and religious people would work hard and do what they were told. They were prepared for a hard journey, would help each other in time of difficulty, and could be relied upon in tight situations.

The gamblers and miners, the dudes from the East, and the dance hall girls would make trouble all the way to Texas.

His suspicions were confirmed later in the day when the group who'd gone to town returned to the campsite. They were drunk and noisy, waving bottles of whisky in the air, riding around the campsite, firing their guns. One was so drunk he fell off his horse.

Stone turned to Taggart. "I think we ought to leave some of these people behind."

"Can't do that," Taggart said. "I'm gittin' paid by the wagon. The less wagons, the less money I make, and if I don't make money, how'm I gonna pay you?"

Everything had been simple in the army. Stone gave orders, and if they weren't carried out, somebody was punished. But these were civilians, difficult to handle.

One of the farmers approached and asked Taggart if he'd help him with a loose wheel, and Taggart departed with him, leaving Stone alone. It was another bright day, with the sun shining in a cloudless sky. Stone felt like going to town and getting a drink of whisky but didn't want to tempt fate. The boys from the Rafter K might be there, and he might not be so lucky this time.

Young Alice McGhee walked toward him. "Is Mister Taggart around?" she asked, wearing a bonnet to shield her eyes from the sun.

"He's just gone to the Royster wagon."

"One of our horses is limping. Think you could take a look at him?"

Stone stood and put on his hat. He walked across the open space with Alice McGhee, aware of her supple young body next to him.

"It was nice to see you at the prayer meeting this morning," she said.

"Your father preaches a hell of a sermon."

"He believes in the power of God, and I was glad to see that you do, too."

Stone smiled politely even though he wasn't sure what he believed in anymore. They came to the McGhee wagon, and the Reverend Joshua McGhee stood beside one of his horses. "Something wrong with his leg," he said.

Stone lifted the horse's leg and looked at the shoe. It was cracked and coming loose.

"Got an extra shoe?"

"I'll get one out of the back," Reverend McGhee said.

Reverend McGhee climbed into the rear of the wagon and rustled around in the boxes. Stone stood beside the big horse and patted his neck.

"I call him Lou," Alice said.

"Hello, Lou," Stone said to the horse.

"I think he's just beautiful."

Reverend McGhee climbed out of the back of his wagon, carrying a hammer, some nails, and a horseshoe. Stone turned his back to the horse, bent over, and held the horse's hoof between his legs. McGhee handed Stone the hammer, and Stone ripped the broken shoe away, then hammered the new shoe firmly in place.

Stone stepped back. The horse whinnied and moved a few steps. He wasn't limping anymore.

"I'm much obliged to you," Reverend McGhee said.

Stone opened his shirt pocket and took out the picture of Marie. "Ever see this woman, Reverend?"

Reverend McGhee squinted his eyes as he looked at the picture. "Can't say that I have." He handed the picture to his wife. "How about you, Doris?"

Doris McGhee accepted the picture. "No, I don't think so. Who is she?"

"Friend of mine."

"She's very pretty, whoever she is."

Stone tucked the picture back into his pocket. He was halfway back to Taggart's wagon when he heard somebody running behind him. Turning, he saw Miss Daisy Sommers, one of the dance hall girls. She had blond hair and a big ass.

"Mister Stone," she said. "We've got our wagon packed and wonder if you'd look at it to make sure it's all right."

He walked beside her toward the wagon. A few times her hips touched his.

"I saw you talkin' to that McGhee girl," Daisy said. "I think she's sweet on you."

Stone didn't know what to say. Daisy looked sideways at him.

"Can't say I blame her. Yer the best lookin' man on this wagon train."

They came to the wagon owned by the dance hall girls. Miss Bottom stood in front. "Glad you could come, Captain Stone," she said. "Would you just crawl in back here and take a look?"

Stone climbed into the back of the wagon, and the three women followed him inside. The trunks and crates were lashed to the sides of the wagon, and he checked the tension of the ropes and security of the knots. "You've done fine," he said.

The four of them were confined to the narrow space in back of the wagon. "Care for a drink?" Miss Bottom asked.

"Don't mind if I do."

Miss Shirley Clanton pulled a bottle from between two trunks and held it in the air, a smile on her pretty face. She handed him the bottle, and he pulled the cork out, raised it in the air, and took a swig.

"Have some more," Miss Bottom said.

"No, that's enough."

He handed the bottle back to Shirley Clanton. Miss

Bottom leaned forward and touched his right knee. "I hope you're not mad at us for the other night."

"I'm not mad at you."

"It's hard for three women travelin' alone. We don't want no special favors or anythin' like that, but we'd appreciate it if you'd look in on us from time to time."

Stone pulled the picture of Marie out of his shirt pocket. "Ever see this woman?"

They passed the picture around, shaking their heads.

"She your wife?" Shirley Clanton asked.

"Friend of mine."

"Real purty."

Stone returned the picture to his shirt pocket.

"You don't have to leave yet," Miss Bottom said.

"Yes, I do," Stone said.

He jumped out of the wagon and walked across the field to Taggart's wagon. Taggart was there, smoking a cigar.

"Where the hell were you?" Taggart asked.

"I put a shoe on the McGhee's horse, and then I looked at the load in one of the other wagons."

"Which wagon was that?"

"The dance hall girls."

"Figured you'd get around to that wagon sooner or later."

"The load was secure. They did a good job."

"I bet they did. Have a little party?"

"Just a drink."

"Don't get too friendly with them dance hall girls. You saw what happened the other night. They're liable to give you somethin' you don't want. I wouldn't want to lose my scout to some strange disease."

Stone boiled water and shaved in his old cracked mirror. Then it was time for supper. He and Taggart had beans and bacon again.

"When we get out on the open trail, we'll hunt for fresh meat," Taggart said. "You ever eat buffalo?"

"No."

"Nothin' like a buffalo steak. It's a little like bear. You've eaten bear?"

"No."

"We'll have to git you some. Rattlesnake stew ain't bad, either."

Night came to the encampment, and Taggart built a bonfire. He'd announced that he wanted to speak with the travelers collectively before they left for Texas in the morning.

The farm families arrived first and sat down in front, close to the bonfire. Then the others drifted toward the fire in twos and threes. Taggart was anxious to begin but noticed some of the travelers weren't there.

"Git the miners, the gamblers, and the dudes from the East," Taggart said to Stone.

Stone pulled his hat firmly on his head and walked toward the miners' wagon. The closer he got, the worse it smelled. He approached the rear and shouted, "Hello in there!"

The curtain in back was pulled to the side, and Joe Doakes stuck his head outside. He was still drunk from his trip to town. "What you want?"

"Time for the meeting."

"What meetin'?"

"Mister Taggart wants to talk to all of you one last time before we pull out in the morning."

"I don't feel like listenin' to that old windbag."

"Don't care how you feel. Let's go."

The barrel of a rifle appeared over the edge of the wagon gate. "Get the hell walkin'," said the voice of Wayne Collins, the moon-faced miner. "We've had just about enough of your shit."

"Think you'd better put that rifle away."

"Hit the trail, cowboy. We ain't goin' to no damn meetin'."

Stone held out his hands and smiled. "Okay."

He walked away, and the curtain dropped over the rear of the wagon. A peal of laughter arose from inside. Stone circled around, ducked into the shadows, and returned to the miners' wagon on his tiptoes. Silently he approached the rear of the wagon and heard a voice inside.

"I guess I showed that big son of a bitch who's boss and who ain't," Collins said.

"Ain't nothin' like a loaded rifle to bring a man back to his senses," Georgie Saulnier replied.

Stone moved to the rear of the wagon, pulled out one of his pistols, and pushed the curtain aside, pointing his pistol at the nose of Collins.

"Let's go to the meeting," Stone said.

Collins turned down the corners of his mouth. "Why, you sneaky son of a bitch!"

Stone pulled the trigger, and his pistol fired. The wagon filled with smoke, and the lobe of Collins' ear blew away, blood spattering in all directions.

"He shot me!" Collins screamed, his round moon face corded with horror. "He shot me!"

"I'll shoot you again if you don't come out of that wagon."

Collins untied his bandanna from his neck and pressed it against his bleeding ear. Georgie Saulnier, with trembling hands, let down the tailgate. He jumped down, followed by Joe Doakes. Collins was last, whimpering like a dog. Stone kicked him in the ass, and Collins went sprawling.

"You aim a rifle at me again," Stone said, "and I'll kill you. That goes for all of you. I'm not playing with you boys anymore. From now on, you either do as you're told, or else. Now move it out."

The three miners made their way across the field, heading toward the bonfire on the other side. Stone walked past the row of wagons until he came to the one inhabited by Tad Holton and Sam Drake, the gamblers. He saw a kerosene lamp flickering inside the canvas and the shadowy shapes of two men. Stone moved to the rear of the wagon and looked inside. No curtain hid the interior, and he saw the two men sitting on the bed of their wagon, playing blackjack.

They looked up as Stone drew closer. Tad Holton wore a rumpled suit and vest with a string tie, while Sam Drake had on his suit pants and a dirty shirt without a vest or tie. They both were in their forties and looked as if they'd been around the frontier a long time.

"Care to sit in?" Holton asked Stone. Holton had a pencil-thin mustache and the sunburn on his face was peeling.

"No thanks," Stone said. "You heard about the meeting?"

"What meetin'?" asked Drake, who wore a goatee and was fat as a pig.

"Captain Taggart's holding a final meeting, and he wants everybody to attend."

Holton looked at Stone and smiled. "Tell you what, friend. Why don't you attend the meeting for us, and then come back and tell us what he said."

"Don't have time for that."

"Don't have time for the meeting."

Stone yanked out both his pistols. "Let's move it out, boys."

Holton held the ace of spades in his hand and froze when he saw the pistol. "Now wait just a goddamn minute!"

Stone pulled the trigger, and a hole appeared in the middle of the spade. Holton stared at it, aghast.

"What time did you say that meeting was starting?" Holton asked.

"It's starting right now."

"We'd better get a move on."

Holton and Drake climbed down from the wagon. They grinned and winked at Stone, then walked swiftly toward the bonfire on the other side of the campsite.

Stone holstered his pistol and walked around the perimeter of the campsite to the oldest, most ramshackle wagon on the train. This was the one belonging to the four dudes from the East: Leary, Maxsell, Hodge, and Tramm. As Stone approached, he heard a fiddle playing. No curtain was strung over the back of the wagon, and he saw the four dudes sprawled around, with Tramm playing the fiddle.

"Howdy boys," Stone said. "Going to the meeting?"

Maxsell raised his hand in the air, and in his hand was a bottle of whisky. "Have a drink," he said.

Stone climbed into the wagon, and all he could smell was whisky. The four dudes were drunk out of their minds. He accepted the bottle, took a swig, and tossed the bottle over his shoulder. It fell to the ground and crashed into tiny pieces.

A hurt expression appeared on Maxsell's face. "Hey, friend, what you do that for?"

"You boys have got yourselves a little too drunk."

"A man's got to have his whisky."

"There's a meeting going on, and you don't want to miss it, so let's go."

Maxsell shook his head. "What the hell we have to go to the meetin' for?"

Stone moved toward him, lifted him up, and pitched him out the rear of the wagon. Maxsell somersaulted through the air and landed on his back.

"Let's go," Stone said to the other three.

"We're a-comin'!" said Tramm.

Hodge, Tramm, and Leary climbed down from the wagon and headed toward the bonfire. Maxsell followed, rubbing his sore ass. Stone was a few steps behind Maxsell, thinking that he definitely didn't want to be coping with drunks for the entire journey to Texas.

They came closer to the blazing fire, and light flickered on the faces of the people gathered around it. Stone looked up and saw a few patches of cloud covering the stars. Taggart stood near his wagon, smoking a cigar. "Everybody here?" he asked.

"Everybody's here," Stone said.

"What was the shootin' I heard?"

"Nothing important."

Taggart rubbed his hands together. "We might as well get started."

Taggart sauntered to the front of the assembly. The farmers and their families waited intently for what he had to say, while the drunks and loafers congregated in back, grumbling and spitting. Collins grimaced as he pressed his filthy bandanna against what remained of his ear.

Taggart held up his hands to quiet everybody down. He wore his wide-brimmed hat, and the reflection of the fire illuminated his ruddy features.

"First thing tomorrow morning, we're movin' out," Taggart said. "We'll want to get an early start so we can cover as much ground as possible, and that'll go for every day we're on the trail, so I'll expect you to cooperate. We'll all git up at dawn every day, and there can't be no exceptions to the rule.

"It's gonna be a long, hard trip. We'll be passin' through country where there's Injuns, outlaws, wild animals, and you-name-it. Our only hope is to stay together and help each other. There might come a time when we have to fight for our lives. All I can say is you'd better make every shot count.

"A wagon train works best when there's only one man in charge, and everybody else does what he says. I'm the man in charge, and what I say goes. We can't all be pullin' in different directions whenever there's trouble. I told you this before when you all signed up, but I want to tell you again. *I give the orders.* That don't mean that I don't wanna hear your suggestions. If we have time, we'll talk things over. But when it comes right down to it, *I give the orders.*"

Taggart continued his lecture, talking about terrain, supplies, the formation of the wagon train, etc. Stone stood with his arms crossed, his eyes roving back and forth over the people in the audience. He wondered how many of them would be alive when they arrived in Texas.

His eyes fell on Alice McGhee, listening intently to what Taggart said. She'd make a good wife for some lucky man, take care of his house, and give him plenty of babies.

He looked back toward the miners, the gamblers, and the city slickers. If there was any trouble on the trail, Stone expected it from them.

Taggart was finishing up his lecture. "We've been gettin' to know each other these past few days," he said, "and in the days to come we're gonna get to know each other a damn sight better. I hope we like each other, but if we don't, we have to get along and work with each other anyways, because we'll all be dependin' on each other out there on the plains. If we work together, we'll all get to Texas in one piece. Any questions?"

The people looked at each other, but nobody said anything. Taggart turned to Stone. "You got anything to say, Captain?"

Stone shook his head.

Taggart faced the group once more, and Reverend Joshua McGhee's hand went up.

"Yes, Reverend?"

"I wonder if I might say a little prayer for all of us."

"I've no objection."

Reverend McGhee stood up, and his wife and daughter gazed at him proudly as he took off his hat and clasped his hands together. He was bald and wore long chin whiskers and no mustache. "Dear Lord," he said, "please safeguard us on our journey through your great plains. Please bless us and keep us, and make Your face shine upon us. You have brought us together, and we have confidence that You'll lead us to our promised land, just like the Israelites. Thank You for the blessings You have already showered upon us, Lord. Thy will be done. Amen."

Reverend McGhee prayed silently for a few moments, then sat down. The people around him unclasped their hands and opened their eyes.

"Anybody else got anything to say?"

No hands went up.

"All right," Taggart said. "Let's turn in and get a good night's sleep, because we want to make an early start tomorrow."

The people got to their feet and slapped the grass and dust from their britches or dresses. They dispersed across the campsite, and Taggart walked back to Stone.

"I seen Mister Collins holding his bandanna against the side of his face," Taggart said, "and it looked like he was bleedin'. What'd you do to him?"

"I shot his ear off."

Taggart blinked in disbelief. "What you do that for?"

"To convince him to come to the meeting."

"Yer awful quick to use them guns of yer'n, but one of these days, somebody's liable to sneak up behind you and shoot you in the back."

"He'd be doing me a favor," Stone said.

"Do me a favor, will you? Stay out of trouble until we get this wagon train to Texas."

The bonfire died down. Stone unrolled his blanket a short distance away and set up his saddle for a pillow. Taggart crawled into the wagon and groaned as he lay down. Stone sat on his blanket and smoked a cigarette. One by one, the lanterns went out in the wagons.

The only sound was wood crackling in the firepit. Stone smoked his cigarette to the butt and threw it into the fire. Then he lay down and covered himself with the blanket. As he fell asleep, he thought, *I'm going to Texas.*

5

BREAKFAST FIRES BURNED and sputtered as the first glimmer of dawn appeared on the horizon. The electricity of anticipation was in the air. Soon the wagon train would begin its long journey toward Texas.

Taggart fried bacon and boiled coffee, and the combination of fragrances cheered Stone's heart. He walked down to the stream and splashed water on his face, joining other travelers who already were there.

The glowing, molten sun rose in the sky, casting long shadows across the campsite as Stone ate a hearty breakfast with Taggart.

"Gonna be a great day," Taggart said. "Can feel it in my bones. Yer to ride in advance of us, but never get out of sight. We'll want to see you, and you'll want to see us. It's big country out there, and easy to get separated."

They finished breakfast, and it was Stone's turn to wash the dishes. Then he saddled his horse and rode it back to the wagon, tethering it to the tailgate. The horse had grown fatter from rest and continual grazing on grass rich in nutrients. It was raring to go.

Taggart and Stone loaded their goods into the wagon, and Taggart sat on the front seat. He slapped the reins against the horses' asses, and the wagon moved out toward the western side of the campsite. Taggart let the wagon pass the edge of the campsite and continue for an additional two hundred yards, then reined in the horses.

Stone rode beside Taggart, and his horse pranced around as if on parade.

"Tell the others to line up behind me," Taggart said.

Stone galloped off, and when he came to the first wagon, he told the Donahue family to fall in behind Taggart. Then Stone rode on to the next wagon, where the McGhees were waiting, and gave them the same orders. Stone proceeded from wagon to wagon, and everybody was ready, smiles on their faces.

They were embarking on a great adventure, and they all knew it. One by one, the wagons formed a long line behind Taggart. Dogs yelped and children sang songs as they gazed over the tailgates.

Stone felt optimistic, as though one chapter in his life was ending and a brand new chapter was beginning. His horse galloped along, and he sat erectly in the saddle, the morning breeze cooling his face.

Finally all the wagons were lined up. Stone rode to the lead wagon and reined his horse in. "We're all set to go," he told Taggart.

Taggart stood on his seat and looked back over the top of his wagon. He saw the long line behind him, the sun gleaming on the canvas that covered the wagons. Taggart raised his arm in the air and pointed it west.

"Wagons ho!" he roared.

Taggart dropped to his seat and slapped the reins on the haunches of his horses. They strained against their harnesses and pulled the wagon forward. Stone spurred his horse and rode off at an angle so he could see the wagon train moving out. One by one, the wagons edged forward, and soon they all were moving. It was a beautiful sight. At last the wagon train was on its way to Texas.

Stone's horse felt the excitement and became frisky. The horse raised its forelegs into the air, pawed around, and then dropped down again. Stone spurred the horse toward the second wagon, where the Donahues were riding.

Stewart Donahue sat on the front seat with his hands

on the reins. His shirtsleeves were rolled up and his massive forearms could be seen. His wife, Martha, wearing a bonnet, sat beside him.

"Everything all right so far?" Stone asked.

"Jest fine," Stewart Donahue replied.

Stone rode back to the next wagon, where the three McGhee's were seated at the front of their wagon, and Alice was closest to Stone.

"Any problems?" Stone asked.

"Not yet," the Reverend Joshua McGhee said.

Stone felt Alice's intense gaze. He looked at her, and she smiled. Wheeling his horse, he rode back to the next wagon.

Everything was rolling along fine. Even the old rickety wagons belonging to the dance hall girls and the dudes from the East were holding together.

The last wagon of the train contained the miners, and Wayne Collins held the reins, his filthy bandanna tied around his head to cover his mutilated ear. Joe Doakes and Georgie Saulnier sat on either side of him, and they were hung over.

"Don't fall too far behind," Stone told them. "We're counting on you to bring up the rear."

"We'll be here," Doakes said, "mainly 'cause there ain't no place else to go."

Stone spurred his horse, and it galloped up the long row of wagons. Finally he came to Taggart at the front.

"Everything's fine," Stone said to Taggart.

"Ride up ahead there and get started earnin' yer pay. We probably won't have any trouble the first day, but we have to be ready."

Stone prodded his horse, and it trotted ahead of the wagon train. The sun climbed in the sky, shining brightly on the grassy swales. A few clouds like puffy white cotton balls drifted east.

He slowed down his horse when he was three or four hundred yards in advance of the wagon train and turned around in his saddle. He saw the wagon train like a long white snake behind him, sending up a huge cloud of dust.

Such a procession would attract a lot of attention once they got into Indian country. More than one wagon train had disappeared without a trace on the plains.

Stone took his map out of his shirt and looked for the first water hole, figuring they'd reach it sometime during the late afternoon. Putting the map away, he urged his horse forward again, this time at a slow walk so he wouldn't get too far ahead of the wagon train.

The wagon train proceeded into the vast western plains. Stone was struck by the sheer endlessness of the ever-changing terrain. There were flatlands, rolling hills, gorges, valleys, buttes, and ridges. Occasionally in the distance he saw a farmhouse. He wondered what it would be like to live in a remote area with Marie and raise cattle. No wonder people left the congested East to come out here. There was a fabulous feeling of freedom, and the air was pure and sweet.

Stone studied the terrain with the eyes of a soldier and saw many suitable spots where an ambush could be laid. The Indians would have the element of surprise on their side. They also were said to be masters of camouflage.

The sheer, stunning beauty of the land was over-whelming, and the vastness of it staggered his imagination. It seemed impossible that a land could be so huge. And it kept going on and on endlessly.

Stone looked back to make sure he wasn't getting too far ahead of the wagon train. So far it was an easy job, but it wouldn't be easy for long.

The sun blazed in the sky, and at high noon Stone rode back to the wagon train. Taggart sat on the front seat of his wagon, munching a biscuit.

"We stopping for lunch?" Stone asked.

"Got to keep goin' till we reach the river. Climb aboard."

Stone moved his horse closer to the wagon and jumped from one to the other. He tied the horse to a cleat on the wagon, and Taggart handed him the bag of biscuits and a chunk of jerked meat.

Stone gnawed on a biscuit. "When do you think we'll come to Indian country."

"We're in it already. Maybe we ain't seen them, but I bet they damn well seen us."

Stone drank some water and climbed into his saddle. He untied his horse and rode back to check the other wagons. Everything seemed to be going all right; nobody had broken down yet.

Stone couldn't help feeling uncomfortable when he passed the McGhee wagon, because young Alice McGhee continued to give him that long, smoldering look. He wondered if she was even conscious of what she was doing.

Stone rode past all the wagons as dogs barked at him and children waved. Then he turned around and galloped back to Taggart.

"Take the point, Captain Stone!"

Stone pulled his hat tight onto his head, and spurred his horse onward, thinking about what Taggart had said. He couldn't see the Indians, but the Indians could see him. Stone looked at the hills and ravines around him, looking for the telltale movement or shape that would indicate the presence of Indians but didn't see anything.

It was almost like being in the war again, on patrol, and brought back memories of Wade Hampton and Jeb Stuart, and old Troop C of the First South Carolina Cavalry. Stone was armed better than he'd been in the war with his two modern pistols and rifle, but instead of seventy or eighty hard-riding cavalry soldiers, he had a wagon train of farmers, miners, dudes, gamblers, and dance hall girls. He wondered how such a group would perform in a pitched battle. Somehow Stone didn't think they'd do so well.

Finally, late in the afternoon, Stone came to the river. It was overflowing its banks due to the rainstorm of a few days ago, moving along swiftly. Trees grew on both sides of the river, and beyond the trees on the far side were high rock bluffs. Stone took out his map and checked to see where he was. Then he turned around and saw the wagon train coming. There was no point riding back to tell Taggart the river was here. He'd find out soon enough.

Stone rolled a cigarette and lit it. He figured it was around four o'clock in the afternoon. He looked at the valley and river and thought it a nice place to put a cabin. The land nearby would grow anything you planted in it, and there was plenty of grazing for livestock.

The wagon train arrived at the bank of the river. "Go on across," Taggart said. "We'll make camp on the other side."

Stone nudged his horse forward. The animal hesitated at first, then plunged in. The water was icy cold, and Stone felt his legs go numb. He held his rifle in the air as his horse swam to the other side.

The horse's hooves touched bottom, and the horse climbed the far side of the river. Stone surged out of the water, and they came to dry land. He turned the horse around and saw Taggart whacking his horses with the reins.

The team of horses drew his wagon into the river, and it sank down to the floorboards. Taggart yipped and yelled, exhorting the horses to keep moving. They pulled him up on the other side as water poured down from their flanks.

One by one, the other horses crossed the river. Children clapped their hands and shrieked gleefully, and dogs swam across on their own. Finally the last wagon floated over the current. Wayne Collins held his reins grimly, and his two companions looked apprehensively at the rapids. They made it across without any damage and cheered as their horses pulled them up the riverbank on the far side.

"We'll make camp here!" Taggart shouted. "Circle the wagons around! Help 'em out, Stone!"

Stone rode in the midst of the wagons and barked orders as in the days when he commanded old Troop C. The wagons coalesced into a circle and settled down. The travelers freed their horses from their harnesses, watered them, and let them graze. Stone removed his saddle and blanket from his horse and picketed him in the grass. Then he returned to Taggart's wagon.

Taggart still was out with his horses. Stone sat down and looked at the map. Tomorrow they'd continue upriver for several miles, then head southwest through a pass.

After that, according to the map, the country would be wide open for more than a hundred miles.

Taggart returned to the wagon. "Time for supper." He took his pots and pans out of the covered wagon, while Stone walked toward his horse. He rubbed him down with dry grass as the fragrance of pork drifted across the campsite.

"Come and git it!" Taggart shouted.

Stone returned to the wagon, sat on the ground, and ate the usual beans and bacon. He was getting sick of it and hoped they'd shoot fresh meat soon.

After the meal, he helped Taggart clean the dishes and pots. The sun wouldn't go down for a few hours, and Stone wasn't tired. He looked up at the bluffs and wondered if he could climb up there. The view should be stupendous.

"I think I'm going to take a look from the top of the bluffs." Stone said to Taggart.

"Ain't you forgettin' somethin'?" Taggart asked.

"What's that?"

"Yer rifle. I wouldn't go anywheres without it, if I was you."

Stone pulled his rifle from his boot next to his saddle and headed for the bottom of the bluffs. He found a path and climbed it, pausing regularly to look at the surrounding country. Down at the campsite, some of the children whistled and waved to him, and he waved back.

He pushed his way upward and finally made it to the top of the bluff. Now he could see in the other direction, and the rolling plains continued on to the horizon. Stone had read somewhere that the horizon was approximately ten miles away at sea level, so he imagined that the horizon from his viewpoint might be twice that.

He looked back to the country over which they'd traveled that day, and it'd been a good distance. The town of Crawford was far away behind the mists of the horizon. Again, Stone marveled at the vastness of the land. A man could escape civilization and find peace, if that's what he was looking for.

Stone rolled a cigarette and lit it as the sun dropped

lower in the sky. He sat on the ground and thought again of how nice it'd be to live here on the wild frontier, far from the strife and madness of civilization.

An eerie feeling came over him, as if he weren't alone. He turned his head around but didn't see anything except trees and bushes. Dropping onto his belly, he moved his rifle into position to fire. He concentrated his mind and listened for unusual sounds, but didn't hear anything.

He waited a few minutes. Nothing happened, but he couldn't dispel the notion that something or somebody was watching him.

He remembered what Taggart had told him. The Indians would see him before he saw them. He realized the top of the bluffs would provide an ideal observation post for watching wagons coming from the east.

Stone backed up, holding his rifle ready to fire. He came to the path and went down quickly, glancing around to see whether anybody was following him. You could escape from civilization, but you had to worry about Indians.

He made his way to ground level and walked to Taggart's fire. Taggart was sitting beside it, conferring with Jason Fenwick, the prosperous farmer. Taggart looked up as Stone approached.

"We've got a problem," Taggart said, then turned to Fenwick. "You tell him."

Fenwick was heavyset and perspiring. He pushed his hat to the back of his head. "Well," he said, "I went with my family to look at our horses, and when we came back to the wagon, things weren't quite the same as when we left. Somebody'd been through our stuff. It wasn't that obvious, but my wife, Mary, has a good eye for details, and she noticed that certain items had been moved." Fenwick looked to his left and right furtively. "We're carrying a fairly substantial sum of money with us, you know, because we intend to buy land in Texas. I'm afraid somebody on this wagon train tried to steal my money."

Taggart said, "That's a very serious accusation, Mister Fenwick."

"It's the truth, and I thought I'd better tell you about it, since you're the wagonmaster."

Stone asked, "Anything missing?"

"Nothing I could see."

"Don't never leave yer wagon unguarded," Taggart said. "Captain Stone and I'll keep an eye on it."

"I have just about everything I own with me in that wagon. I'd hate to have it stolen."

"We understand how you feel, Mister Fenwick. We'll do everything we can."

Fenwick stood, brushed off the seat of his pants, and walked back to his wagon.

"Nothing worse than havin' thieves in a wagon train," Taggart said. "Makes everybody suspicious of everybody else. Not much we can do about it except keep our eyes open." He puffed his cigar and looked at the top of the bluffs. "You see anythin' interestin' when you were up there?"

"I think I had company."

"Injuns?"

"I didn't see any, but somebody was up there. I could feel them. I know that sounds strange, but it's true."

"It's not so strange. I know the feeling myself. Some people know when danger's around whether they can see it or not. It's a good thing they didn't put an arrow in your ass."

"I think they're watching us right now."

"They probably are. They pay attention to everything that passes through their country."

"Think they'll attack?"

"Hard to say. Depends on how many of them they are and what kind of weapons they have. We'll find out soon enough."

Taggart looked back to the top of the bluffs that made a dim outline against the twilight sky. The sun already was out of sight behind the bluffs. A coyote howled somewhere in the distance, and a night bird squawked.

"Don't you think we should post guards?" Stone asked.

"Injuns don't attack at night, but we might have something to worry about tomorrow."

"You don't seem very worried about it."

"What's there to worry about? I been through this too many times. If the Injuns attack, the onliest thing you can do is fight 'em. There ain't as many Injuns around these days as there used to be, and they ain't never stopped me yet. We might lose some people, but we'll get through all right. We're a pretty big party, you know. The Injuns only attack when they see an easy victory, and this wagon train ain't gonna be no easy victory. Like you said once: Nobody's lookin' to die, not even Injuns."

6

THE WAGON TRAIN moved out early in the morning, following the trail alongside the river, and then it turned west.

The plains rolled toward the horizon, and in all that space there was nothing but the creak of wagons and the pounding of horses' hooves. The sun shone brightly, and Stone rode ahead of the wagons, reconnoitering the country. Shortly before noon he saw clumps of brown bushes covering the plains for miles, but as he observed them more closely, he saw they were moving.

Buffalo. He'd heard about the great herds, and there they were, like a carpet over the terrain, thousands of them. Wheeling his horse, he galloped back to the lead wagon.

"Buffalo!" Stone said to Taggart, pointing to the north. "A whole herd of them. Should I shoot some?"

"I'd better go with you."

Stone raised his hand to stop the wagon train, and the wagons pulled to a halt behind him. Taggart saddled one of the riding horses as Reverend McGhee approached from the rear of the train.

"What're we stopping for, Taggart?"

"Fresh meat. You stay here with the others and wait for us to come back."

Taggart climbed onto his horse and rode with Stone

toward the buffalo. "They got a keen sense of smell," Taggart said. "We've got to approach them from upwind."

They angled their horses toward the upwind side of the herd, and the buffalo grazed peacefully, paying no attention to them.

"That's a lot of buffalo," Stone said.

"This is just a small herd compared to what they used to be. Hunters and rawhiders are killin' 'em all. In another ten or twenty years, there won't be none left. Think we'd better dismount here before we spook 'em."

Stone reined in his horse and climbed down. He and Taggart picketed the horses in a thicket.

"We gotta creep up on 'em real slow and easy," Taggart said. "When I give the word, open fire. Aim right here," he pointed to his left armpit, "that's where their heart is. The main thing is be quiet. We'll shoot as many as we can."

Taggart dropped to his belly and crawled toward the buffalo that were about five hundred yards away. Stone followed, cradling his rifle in his arms. They made their way across the grassy plain and gradually closed the distance between them and the buffalo.

The buffalo had short horns and huge heads covered with woolly hair. Stone thought they were the most freakish-looking creatures he'd ever seen. They mooed like cows and cropped grass peacefully, unaware that death was stalking them.

Taggart stopped moving, turned to Stone, and winked. He pressed the butt of his rifle against his shoulder and took aim. Stone followed his example and lined up his sights on a gigantic buffalo grazing directly in front of him.

Taggart's rifle boomed in the afternoon, and a buffalo in the herd crumpled to its knees. A moment later Stone pulled his trigger, and his buffalo raised its head in surprise. Then the buffalo's knees buckled and it collapsed onto the ground.

The other buffalo raised their heads and sniffed the air. Then they moved away from the gunshot in a rolling brown mass, mooing and hooting. Stone jacked the lever of his rifle and took aim at the rear end of a buffalo just as Taggart fired again. Stone squeezed his trigger, and the rear legs of his buffalo gave out. The buffalo tried to move forward on his front legs alone, and Stone shot it again, and then again. The animal dropped to the ground, coughing blood.

The herd thundered away, streaming over hills and through the long, wide canyons, and the ground shook with the pounding of their hooves. Five buffalo lay motionless on the grass.

Taggart got to his feet. "You stay here with 'em, and I'll go back for the others. We'll have a feast tonight, m'boy."

Taggart walked back to his horse, and Stone advanced to take a closer look at the dead buffalo. They lay on the ground, bleeding from holes in their torsos, their tongues hanging out, and their eyes open and staring. Stone dropped to one knee and rolled a cigarette. How quickly death could come when you least expected it.

It had been like that in the war. You could have a friend, and next day he'd be dead. He'd lost many friends in the war, and after awhile he stopped being friendly.

Something prompted Stone to turn around. A butte was behind him, and he thought he saw a man standing on top of it. Stone blinked his eyes. The man was gone. Had he hallucinated, or did he actually see somebody?

He couldn't be sure. The bright sun and broad vistas were making his eyes play tricks, but he was in Indian country and maybe he'd seen an Indian.

He turned around and saw the wagon train approaching. The line broke apart as the individual wagons approached the ground where the buffalo were lying. Taggart brought his wagon to a stop and jumped down.

"I thought I saw a man on that butte over there," Stone said, pointing.

Taggart turned to look. "If it was an Injun, you wouldn't've seen him at all. Might've been a white man. Might've been a coyote. Hard to say."

The other travelers gathered around the dead buffalo.

The children appeared fascinated. Alice McGhee looked sick.

"Let's skin and butcher 'em," Taggart said.

He yanked out his knife and began cutting, and blood oozed onto the ground. Taggart slit his animal's belly and tore out its liver. He bit off a raw chunk of it, red blood staining his white mustache.

"Best part," he said with satisfaction.

The travelers butchered the buffalo and divided the meat. Then they built fires, because it would last longer cooked.

The campsite took on a festive air as the buffalo were stripped of their skins and meat. Soon only the bloody bones and entrails were left. Fragrant spirals of smoke rose into the sky. Stone figured that the meat ought to last several days, and then, if they were lucky, they'd find another herd.

The travelers enjoyed a big feast of buffalo steaks, then packed the remainder of the cooked meat, loaded it into their wagons, and rolled toward Texas again, leaving the carcasses of the dead buffalo behind.

Stone took the point again, riding in a southwesterly direction. They continued until dark and stopped for the night at the edge of a forest, where they made camp.

Before dawn they were awake again, and it was a cloudy day. They ate buffalo meat and moved out again, advancing steadily across the prairie. They didn't stop for lunch, eating buffalo meat while the wagons rumbled over the rocks and holes in the ground.

In the late afternoon, Stone saw a profusion of trees and vegetation, the water hole where they were supposed to spend the night. He rode ahead to investigate.

It was an island of trees in the middle of a sea of grass. Stone saw no tracks on the ground and no sign of Indians. The trees could conceal a substantial number of them, and Stone drew his rifle out of its scabbard, peering ahead suspiciously.

He rode into the trees, and it was silent and cool. The trees were tall, blocking out the light. Stone followed the trail and came to the water hole, clear as glass. He climbed down from his horse, led it forward, and let it drink as he scrutinized the trees and bushes for shapes or movements that might indicate the presence of Indians. Finding nothing threatening, he took off his hat, lay down, and kissed his lips to the water.

It was sweet and cold, and he gulped it down eagerly. Next to him, his horse slurped noisily.

Stone heard a *thunk* sound next to him. He lurched around and saw an arrow sticking out of the ground only three inches away from his knee. He dived to the ground, pulled out his pistols and cocked the hammers.

It was silent and dark in the grove of trees, but he knew an Indian, or maybe more than one Indian, was out there. That arrow didn't launch itself into the air without help.

He was sure the Indians could see him, but he couldn't see them. He peered into the foliage, but there was nothing. He was a sitting duck, because he'd walked to the water hole without taking precautions. The uneventful day had lulled him into a sense of safety, but there was no safety now. If that arrow had flown a few inches higher, he'd be a dead man. He raised a pistol and fired three shots into the air to warn the wagon train.

The sound of the shots reverberated over the prairie. He couldn't hear the wagon train anymore and assumed it'd stopped. Taggart was wondering what happened.

Stone picked up his rifle and sighted down the barrel. What if the Indians rushed him? All he could do was fight them off as best he could. *What are they waiting for?* He examined the bushes and trees in front of him but couldn't see anything. He wondered if the Indians were still there.

"Hello, Stone!" Taggart shouted in the distance.

"I'm in here!" Stone replied. "Somebody shot an arrow at me!"

"Stay where you are! We'll be right there! Don't shoot any of us by mistake!"

Stone held his rifle tightly and wondered what the Indians were up to. They could kill him easily if there were enough of them, but maybe it was just a lone brave who'd already run off after scaring the white man half to death.

Taggart's head popped up from a bush in front of him. "Are you all right?"

"He missed me."

"If he missed you, maybe he didn't want to hit you."

Taggart stood, his rifle in his hands, and pushed his way out of the bush. He was followed by the Reverend Joshua McGhee, Stewart Donahue, Jason Fenwick, and a few of the others. Stone pulled the arrow out of the ground and held it out to Taggart.

Taggart looked at the feathers at the end of the shank. "Comanche," he said.

The wagons rolled into the grove and formed their defensive circle. The men watered and picketed the horses, and the women prepared supper, but all kept weapons close at hand.

Darkness came to the water hole. Stone and Taggart gnawed on buffalo meat.

"They know where we are," Taggart said. "Wonder what they'll do about it?"

"Maybe they'll attack first thing in the morning."

"They will if they think it'll be easy."

"They almost killed me. Now I know why they say a good Indian is a dead Indian."

"How would you like it if people moved into yer backyard, took yer food, and crowded you out of yer house? They're fightin' back the onliest way they know how. We broke every treaty we ever made with 'em. If yer gonna be livin' out here, you'll have to understand these people, because you'll have to deal with 'em, that's fer damn sure."

A shriek pierced the night air. Stone jumped to his feet, yanked out his six-guns, and ran in the direction of the sound. It came from the other side of the wagons on the far side of the campsite. Other men grabbed their pistols and rifles and ran toward the same area. Stone plunged into the bushes, found a trail, and ran along it. Ahead he saw Miss Bottom, an expression of consternation on her face.

"There was a man in the bushes!" she said. "I was back there at the ladies' latrine, and he was watchin' me."

"Was he an Indian?"

"I don't know."

Miss Bottom led them back to the ladies' latrine, a hole in a small clearing.

"I was over here," she said, pointing at the hole, "and he was over there." She indicated the bushes straight ahead.

Stone moved into the bushes and saw that something or somebody had been there because branches were broken and the earth was stomped down. He got on his hands and knees and ran his fingers over the tracks, feeling the marks of boot soles and heels.

He returned to Miss Bottom. "I'll walk you back to your wagon."

Stone and Miss Bottom headed across the campsite, followed by a group of armed travelers.

"Maybe you shouldn't go to the latrine by yourself anymore," he said. "Take one of the other women with you."

"I think I know who it was."

"I thought you said you didn't see him."

"I know who it was anyway. Mike Leary's been gogglin' at me and makin' remarks. I wouldn't be surprised if it was him."

"I'll have a talk with him."

The other travelers walked back to their wagons. Stone accompanied Miss Bottom to hers, then continued around the circle to the one occupied by the four dudes from the East: Mike Leary, Frank Maxsell, Homer Hodge, and Lou Tramm. He found them lounging around their fire, smoking cigarettes and drinking coffee.

"All four of you been here all evening?" Stone asked.

"What you wanna know fer?" Homer Hodge asked. He was slope-shouldered, gaunt and wore a huge cowboy hat and had acne scars on his face.

"Just answer the question."

"'Course we been here. Where the hell else you think we were?"

Stone looked at Leary. "How about you?"

Leary was small with blond hair like straw. "What're you drivin' at, Stone?"

"You haven't been hanging around the ladies' latrine, have you, Leary?"

"What makes you think it was me?" Leary said indignantly. "Is that what Miss Bottom said? Well, she's lyin'! I don't hang around no ladies' latrines! I got better things to do!"

Stone pointed his finger at Leary. "Don't ever let me catch you over there."

Stone walked back to Taggart's wagon. The air carried the fragrance of smoke from fires burning throughout the campsite. Taggart lay on his back near his fire, his head resting on his saddle, a cigar sticking out the corner of his mouth.

"What was the problem?" he asked.

"Somebody was peeking at Miss Bottom while she was going to the latrine. She thinks it was Mike Leary."

Taggart sighed and shook his head. "There's one on every wagon train."

7

THE WAGON TRAIN passed a farmhouse in the middle of nowhere. The farmer and his family waved at the lone rider in front of the wagon train, and Stone waved back.

The farmer and his oldest sons were all muscle and bone with rugged faces. The woman looked as tough as the men, and the kids seemed happy. They had a vegetable garden, a few cattle, pigs and chickens, and were carving a life for themselves on the American frontier.

A man could start out all over in this bright new land, Stone realized. It didn't matter what you'd done or hadn't done. You could make yourself into anything you wanted, throw off an old identity, make a new one.

Most of the time the travelers saw nothing except the endless expanse of plains, hills, and sky. Stone realized for the first time how huge America was. If a man wanted to get away from it all, this was the place to be.

On the fourth day after the peeping-Tom incident, he saw up ahead a vast mountain range that looked like a barrier across their path. Taking out his map, he saw that the trail was supposed to lead through a narrow pass cut into the mountains.

He couldn't see the pass; it was still too far away. His horse plodded along, and Stone took off his hat, mopping his brow with the back of his shirt sleeve. He lifted his

canteen and took a drink, then turned in the saddle and
saw the white canvas tops of the wagon train behind him.

The mountain barrier came closer. Stone rocked back
and forth in his saddle, holding the reins. He was becoming
lazy, because nothing had happened for the past few days.
He was beginning to think the rest of the trip would be
uneventful. Maybe tomorrow he'd do some hunting. The
wagon train was running low on fresh meat.

In the middle of the afternoon, he approached the mountain range. Stopping his horse, he looked at the map again,
but the map didn't furnish enough particulars about where
the pass was. Stone would have to find it himself. It was
straight ahead, according to the map.

Stone folded his map and put it away, then pulled his
old army compass out of his saddlebag and oriented himself. Next he yanked his army spyglass out of the saddlebag
and scanned the terrain ahead. He saw the opening in the
mountain range. It was toward his left; the wagon train
had been a few miles off course.

Stone angled his horse to the left and dropped his spyglass back into his saddlebag. His horse trudged over the
prairie grass, passing bushes and trees. They were supposed to make camp that night somewhere in the mountains. A stream was there according to the map.

As Stone drew closer to the mountains, he saw the pass
with his naked eyes. It was narrow; not more that two or
three wagons could go through abreast. Then something
caught his eye.

There were figures in front of the pass. Stone took out
his spyglass and focused it straight ahead. He saw five men
with horses a few hundred yards in front of the pass. The
horses were grazing, and the men sat nearby. They weren't
Indians, so Stone thought they must be cowboys, but where
were their cows?

Stone wondered whether to ride on and encounter the
men himself or go back and tell Taggart. He decided to
tell Taggart. Taggart would know what to do.

Stone wheeled his horse and galloped back toward the
wagon train, his horse kicking up clods of earth. The wagon

train came closer, and he saw Taggart in front, his reins wrapped around his hands. Stone slowed his horse as he approached Taggart's wagon.

"Men up ahead!" Stone shouted. "Five of them that I could see."

Taggart's brow furrowed. "Did they look like Injuns?"

"Definitely aren't Indians," Stone replied. "They're white men."

"What were they doin'?"

"Nothing I could see."

"Did they have much supplies or equipment with 'em?"

"Seemed to be traveling light."

"Don't look good," Taggart said. "They ain't travelers like us, and they ain't cowboys because I don't see no cows."

"Maybe they're hunters."

"No buffalo around. Ride back and tell the wimmin and children to git out of sight."

Stone rode back and passed the word along. The men gathered their rifles and pistols, and the women and children climbed into the rear of the wagons, getting low behind the sidewalls.

Stone rode to the side of the wagon train and took out his spyglass. He peered ahead and saw the five men on their horses, strung out in a line in front of the pass, blocking the way.

Stone dropped his spyglass into his saddlebag and spurred his horse. He rode toward Taggart and said, "Looks like they don't want us to go through."

Taggart set his mouth into a grim line. "It's gonna be a holdup."

"We should be able to handle them. They've only got five men."

"There's only five that you can see. What about the ones you can't see?"

Stone hadn't stopped to think there might be more men than the ones he could see. "What'll we do?"

"We'll find out what they want."

The wagon train moved forward, and the five men on

horseback became clearer. They were a dusty bunch in mangled hats and raggedy clothes, all wearing beards. The one in the middle was tall and slim, even taller than Stone, or so it appeared in the distance.

"They're waitin' for us," Taggart said. "Let's you and me go up and palaver with 'em. We'll leave the rest back here for safekeepin'."

Taggart pulled back his reins, and his horses slowed to a halt. The other wagons stopped behind him. He climbed down from his seat and mounted one of the horses tethered to the back of the wagon.

"Let's go," he said to Stone.

Stone and Taggart rode side by side toward the five men, while the travelers watched and wondered what was going on.

Stone and Taggart advanced toward the mountain pass. The five men looked like hard cases who hadn't seen a town in weeks. Two smoked skinny cigarettes, and the tall one in the middle chewed tobacco, spitting a huge brown gob at the ground as Stone and Taggart came abreast of them.

The tall man's lips were ringed with brown tobacco juice. "It'll cost you five hundred dollars to git yer wagons through that there pass behind me."

"What if I don't pay?" Taggart asked.

"You don't go through." He aimed his thumb at the mountains behind him. "I got men with rifles up there. You won't make it. Take my word for it."

"You drive a hard bargain."

"Tough shit."

"I'll have to go back and talk with my people about it."

"Talk all you want, but let's get one thing straight. There ain't no way yer gettin' through this pass in one piece less'n you pay me five hundred dollars. You try it, we won't have no mercy. Wimmin and children don't mean a fuck-all to us. You get what I'm sayin'?"

"I hear you," Taggart said.

Taggart and Stone headed back toward the wagons.

When they were out of earshot of the highwaymen, Taggart leaned toward Stone.

"I reckernize 'em," he said. "They're the Owsley Gang. They used to ride with Bloody Bill Anderson's guerrilla cavalry durin' the war. After it ended, they come out here, and they're doin' pretty much the same thing they done in Missouri and Kansas: robbin', rapin', and killin' civilians. Unless I miss my guess, that tall one's Hank Owsley hisself. I saw his picture in a sheriff's office once, and it damn sure looks like him."

They rode back to the wagon train, and Taggart dismounted behind his wagon.

"All right everybody!" Taggart said. "Let's have a meetin'!"

He walked off to the side of the wagon train and sat on the grass. Stone sat beside him, glancing back at the five outlaws poised like sentinels at the entrance to the pass. He looked up to the mountains and wondered if the outlaws were bluffing. Did they really have men with rifles up there, and if so, how many?

The travelers gathered around Taggart and Stone. There were the McGhees and the Donahues, the Fenwicks and the Roysters, gamblers, city slickers, miners, kids, and dogs. The men held their rifles and looked suspiciously at the five men guarding the entrance to the pass.

"What's goin' on?" asked Sam Drake, the gambler with the goatee.

"We got a problem," Taggart said. "Them's outlaws up there, and if we don't give 'em five hundred dollars, they won't let us go through the pass."

Georgie Saulnier spat into the grass. "Sheet," he said, "that ain't no problem. They's only five of 'em."

"You only *see* five of 'em, Georgie," Taggart replied, "but they got more in the mountains, with rifles. At least that's what they said."

Reverend McGhee cleared his throat and spoke in his deep, resonant voice. "Do we have to use this pass, Taggart? Can't we go around some other way?"

"We could, but we might have to travel a few hundred

miles out of our way through uncharted wilderness that's infested with Injuns, and I don't know where the water is. Them outlaws got us over a barrel. They know we need to use this pass."

Maxsell, one of the dudes from the East, pulled out his six-gun and grinned. "Can't we fight 'em off? Hell, I'd rather fight than give 'em all that money."

"How're you gonna fight 'em?" Taggart asked. "They're hidden in the mountains. The way I see it, we got four choices. We can pay them their money. We can go the long way and take our chances. We can go back the same way we came. Or we can make a run for it through the pass and hope for the best."

"I wouldn't recommend that last one," Stone said. "If they've got men up there as they say, they'd cut us down like fish in a barrel."

"I don't think we should give in to them," Donahue said. "I think we should go the long way around."

Taggart shrugged. "That's liable to cost us more than five hundred dollars in the long run, because it'll add additional time to the trip, and time is money. I don't know what's on that route and couldn't guarantee we'll get through. It might be impassable."

Holton, the gambler with the pencil-thin mustache, leaned forward. "What if they take our money and shoot us down anyways?"

"If they attacked us, we'd fight back, and they know some of them'd git hurt, too. I think them outlaws is lazy. A fast five hundred dollars is what they want." He looked at Stone. "What do you think?"

Stone had been considering the problem from a military point of view while the others had been talking, and he thought the outlaws held all the high cards. They occupied the best terrain and could fight off attackers indefinitely. It was like the pass at Thermopylae in ancient Greece where a handful of Spartans held off the Athenian army.

"I think we should pay them," Stone said, "and go through the pass."

"I just thought of somethin'," said Wayne Collins, his

mangled ear hanging on one side of his head. "How do we know you ain't in cahoots with 'em?"

Taggart turned to him solemnly. "What was that?"

"Maybe we'll pay five hundred dollars, and they'll split it with you. Maybe that's why you're a-tellin' us to pay the money, because it's gonna wind up in yer own pocket afterwards."

Taggart pulled out his six-gun and pointed it at Collins. "If yer callin' me a crook, we're a-gonna havta fight it out. Go for yer gun."

Collins became agitated. "Wait a minute, now. I was just raisin' the issue, that's all. Don't be a-gittin' hot under yer collar."

Taggart continued pointing his pistol at him. "You call a man a crook in this country—you'd better be ready to fight."

"Don't get yer feathers riled," Collins said. "I'm sorry."

Taggart holstered his gun and sat down. "Let's come to a decision, folks. We don't have all day."

"Why don't we have all day?" Joe Doakes asked. "What's the hurry?"

"I don't want to be out here at night with those outlaws up in the mountains."

Fenwick said, "I agree with Captain Stone. We should pay the money because we don't have much choice. Split among us, it won't be that much."

Hodge, one of the dudes from the East, looked at Fenwick sullenly. "Maybe it won't be much to *you*, but it might be a lot to the rest of us."

Fenwick blushed, because he was the richest man on the wagon train and everybody knew it. A few of the others shifted their positions uneasily. Miss Bottom was the next to speak.

"I think we should pay it," she said. "Them outlaws got us where they want us, and the sooner we realize it, the better off we'll be."

"We'll take a vote," Taggart said, "and whatever the majority decides, that's what we'll do. Everybody who thinks we should pay off the outlaws, raise yer hands."

Most of the hands went up.

"Who don't want to pay the outlaws?"

No hands went up.

"Some of you didn't vote," Taggart said. "Why the hell not?"

"I don't know what to do," Wayne Collins said.

"The majority rules. You folks figger out how much each of you has to pay."

"Whataya mean, each of us?" Collins said. "What about you?"

"Me and Stone don't pay," Taggart said. "We're just along for the ride."

The travelers grumbled as they returned to their wagons to get the money. Some had it in strongboxes, others in money belts, others hidden in special secret places. One by one they returned with the money and dropped it into Taggart's hat.

Taggart rose and hitched up his gunbelts. "Let's go pay the bastards," he said to Stone.

Taggart and Stone climbed onto their horses and rode toward the outlaws.

"We got your money," Taggart said as they approached.

"Hand it over," said the tall thin man with tobacco juice on his lips, the one Taggart had said was Hank Owsley.

Taggart rode forward and handed his hat to Owsley, who dismounted and counted the money.

"It's all there," Taggart said.

"It'd better be."

Owsley fingered the last coin and growled, "You and your nesters can use the pass now. You'd better git goin' afore we change our minds."

Stone gazed down at him. "What do you mean—change your mind?"

Owsley smiled, revealing rotted stumps of teeth. "We got a deal as long as I don't change my mind. That's the way it is, cowboy."

In a movement so fast his hand was a blur, Stone pulled out his six-gun and pointed it at Owsley, whose eyes widened like saucers.

"Where I come from," Stone said, "a deal is a deal."

Owsley's smile disappeared from his face. "Put that gun away, if you know what's good for you."

"You're comin' with us, Owsley, to make sure we get through the pass without you changing your mind about our deal."

"Now, just a moment . . ."

"Get on your horse, or you're a dead son of a bitch."

Owsley smiled again. "I was only kiddin' about changin' my mind. You don't have to get all persnickety about it."

"Get on your horse."

Owsley looked at his men, and they all knew they were in a predicament. They outnumbered Stone and Taggart, but Owsley would be killed without question if there were gunplay.

"Okay-okay," Owsley said, getting to his feet. "Some fellers can't take a joke, I guess."

One of Owsley's henchmen spoke. He had a gray beard and wore a black hat with the front brim turned up. "What about the money?" he asked Owsley.

"What about it?"

"Don't you think you'd better leave it with us—fer safe-keepin'? Otherwise they got you, they got the money, and we let them go through the pass. Sounds to me like there's somethin' wrong with that deal."

Owsley turned to Stone. "How do I know you'll turn me loose after we get through the pass?"

"You've got my word, and I don't change my mind like you."

"So now I gotta trust you."

"We've got to trust each other is the way I see it."

Owsley gave the money to the gray-bearded outlaw. "Let's get this thing over with," he said to Stone.

"Hand over your gun, handle first," Stone said, "and do it real slow."

Owsley spat tobacco juice onto the ground, and an evil

glint came to his eye. He hesitated for a moment, then drew his pistol and handed it to Stone handle first.

"You're lucky today," Owsley said. "Another day maybe you won't be so lucky."

"Ride back to those wagons, and don't make any funny moves."

"You're makin' me mad, cowboy."

"Ride on, and shut up."

Owsley spurred his horse. Stone and Taggart followed him, leaving the four outlaws behind.

"By the way," Stone hollered over his shoulder at them, "you boys try anything at all, and Hank Owsley's a dead man!"

Stone, Taggart, and Owsley rode back to the wagons, and Stone kept his pistol pointed at Owsley's back. Owsley was affecting a nonchalant attitude.

"Looks like a Confederate campaign hat yer wearin'," Owsley told Stone. "I rode for the Confederacy myself."

"The Confederacy I rode for didn't kill women and children and steal everything that wasn't nailed down."

They returned to the wagon train, and the settlers were waiting, their rifles in their hands.

"Who the hell's that?" asked Georgie Saulnier.

"Don't matter who he is," Taggart replied. "Mount up your wagons. We're a-goin' through the pass."

"He one of them outlaws?" Saulnier said.

"He is."

Saulnier aimed his rifle at Owsley. "Why don't we shoot him and git it over with?"

"Because if we shoot him, we won't get through the pass, and on top of that, we'll have a war on our hands, so put down yer rifle and get on yer damned wagon."

Saulnier lowered his rifle. They all trudged back to the wagons.

"Keep the wimmin and children out of sight!" Taggart shouted. "You men—git ready for anythin'!"

Stone, Taggart, and Owsley tied their horses to the back of the wagon, then climbed onto the front seat. Owsley sat between Stone and Taggart, and Stone pointed his pistol at Owsley's head. "You'd better not try anything."

"I ain't a-gonna try anythin', cowboy. Just make sure you don't fire that thing by mistake."

Stone recoiled from Owsley's fetid breath. Owsley chewed his tobacco and spit a wad between the rumps of the horses. Tagggart turned around and looked at the wagon train. Everybody was ready to go. He moved his arm forward.

"Wagons ho!"

He flicked the reins in his hands, and the horses moved forward. The wagon rocked from side to side as it traversed the prairie, and Stone kept his pistol pointed at Owsley's head. The rest of the wagon train followed behind Taggart, and they all headed for the narrow pass in the mountains.

The outlaws at the front of the pass were out of sight now. Stone guessed they'd taken their positions in the mountains. The path was clear, and the wagon train rolled inexorably toward the pass.

Stone looked up to the cliffs and ridges and saw the glint of sun on gunmetal. Owsley's men were up there, watching the wagon train pass through. They held the best terrain, and they'd earn five hundred dollars without firing a shot.

Taggart's wagon entered the narrow, winding pass. Stone recalled from his map that the pass continued for about a half mile, then opened onto a vast basin. Stone hoped they made it to the basin without any trouble. The outlaws in the mountains could pick them off easily with rifles if they wanted to.

Stone realized Owsley wasn't as dumb as he looked. If he and his men had simply massacred the wagon train, they'd bring the law or the cavalry down on them. A little extortion was less likely to draw attention from the authorities.

The wagon train made its way through the narrow pass. In some sections, there wasn't enough room for two wagons to move side by side. The travelers looked up fearfully at the rocky crags and saw rifle barrels and the outlines of cowboy hats against the clear blue sky.

The confining dimensions of the pass caused sound to echo off the rock. Equipment rattled in the wagons, wheels ground against stone, and the shod hooves of horses pounded on the ground. All the travelers expected shots to ring out at any moment. Anxiety mounted with every passing minute.

Taggart led the wagon train through the twists and turns of the mountain pass, while Stone continued to point his gun at Owsley, who appeared unconcerned by what was going on. As they neared the end of the pass, Owsley turned toward Stone. "I can pay you more than them nesters," he said. "Why don't you throw in with me?"

"I'm not a crook."

Owsley laughed. "You want to be a good feller, huh? Well, you know where good fellers wind up. They die broke and get thrown into Boot Hill. Is that what you want?"

"I don't care what happens to me," Stone said.

The pass widened ahead, and Stone could see the immense basin spread out beyond it. Taggart urged his horses on, and they pulled the wagon out of the pass.

"We made it!" Taggart said.

The lead wagon rolled on, and the rest of the wagon train followed it onto the basin. They continued for a few hundred yards, and then Taggart raised his hand to stop the wagon train. The horses slowed down and the wagons creaked to a halt.

A faint breeze blew. Stone continued to point his pistol at Owsley's head.

"Jump down," Stone said.

Owsley climbed down from the wagon, and Stone followed him, maintaining his aim at Owsley's head.

"Untie your horse," Stone told him.

They walked to the rear of the wagon, and Owsley untied his horse. Some of the travelers appeared, carrying their rifles. Tad Holton and Sam Drake, the two gamblers, were leading them. Taggart joined Stone at the rear of the wagon.

"You ain't gonna let him go, are you?" Holton asked Stone.

"That was the deal," Stone said.

"To hell with the deal. We oughta hold him for ransom until his pals give us our money back."

Owsley scowled. "Now jest a minute!"

Holton tucked his rifle barrel under Owsley's chin. "No, *you* wait jest a minute." Holton's pencil-thin mustache quivered with emotion. "We'll do with him what we damn well please."

Owsley looked at Stone and Taggart. "We had a deal," he reminded them.

"Get on yer horse," Taggart said.

"Hold on," said Sam Drake, the other gambler, pointing his rifle at Taggart.

Taggart's face turned red. "Point that rifle the other way!" he commanded.

Drake saw the fire in Taggart's eyes and backed off. He aimed his rifle to the ground. "I don't think we should let him go," he said weakly. "He stole five hundred dollars of our money."

"I know what he did," Taggart replied, "but he ain't alone. He's got men back there, and we don't know how many they are. If we kill him, we'll have to contend with them. They ain't gonna just walk away if we kill him. So we're lettin' him go. A deal's a deal."

Owsley climbed onto his horse. "My gun," he said to Stone.

Stone threw it at him, and Owsley caught it in the air.

"Put it in your holster real slow," Stone said. "You don't want to make me nervous, because I might pull this trigger."

Owsley grinned as he holstered his piece. "That good enough?" he asked.

"Start riding, and don't look back."

Owsley stared at Stone. "We're gonna meet again someday, cowboy, and when we do, I'll even up the score."

"I said start riding."

Owsley spurred his horse, and the travelers watched him head back toward the mountains.

"You shouldn't've let him go," Tad Holton said to Taggart.

"He kept his side of the deal, and we kept our side."

"But we're out five hundred dollars."

"You coulda been out your life."

Holton narrowed his eyes. "There's something fishy about this. I hate to bring it up again, but somebody's got to. How do we know you're not in on the deal with the outlaws?"

There was silence for a few moments. The travelers were gathered around, holding their rifles, and some looked confused. Stone kept his eyes on Owsley to make sure the outlaw wasn't going to try something foolish, like taking a shot at them with his rifle, but Owsley still rode toward the mountains.

Taggart said, "This is the second time somebody accused me of bein' in cahoots with them outlaws. The next time somebody says it, I'm a-gonna kill him."

Nobody said anything. A few of the travelers shifted their feet nervously. Tad Holton went pale, and Taggart looked him in the eye. Holton couldn't take it and turned in another direction.

The travelers glanced at each other and grumbled. They didn't like the idea of losing five hundred dollars but didn't know what to do about it.

Stone was irritated by the way Owsley and his gang had stolen five hundred dollars from innocent people, most of them poor. He remembered Owsley's rotted teeth and stinking breath. He didn't like him.

"We might as well git movin' along," Taggart said. "No use cryin' over spilt milk. Mount up yer wagons and let's move out. Captain Stone—take the point."

Stone climbed onto his horse. He took out his map, and there was a lake straight ahead about five miles away. That's where they were scheduled to camp for the night. He spurred his horse and it moved along the old wagon trail. He wondered how many other wagon trains had been held up by Owsley and his men.

Stone looked behind him and saw the wagon train following the trail. A few clouds drifted across the sky, and buzzards circled lazily overhead. Owsley and his gang earned five hundred dollars in a day, and Stone'd be lucky if he earned sixty dollars for his entire trip to Texas.

He imagined the outlaws in their camp in the mountains. They'd get drunk, sing songs, and go to bed. He wondered how many men Owsley had. Stone didn't think it'd be difficult to track Owsley back to his camp.

Owsley's kind never hesitated to kill when it suited their purposes. If he and his men had ridden with Bloody Bill Anderson's guerrilla cavalry, they'd probably massacred men, women, and children.

In the distance, Stone saw the lake shimmering in the sun. His horse pricked up his ears; he could smell the water. Walking more quickly, he was anxious to get his snout into it. Stone patted him on the mane and wondered if he should go back and try to retrieve the money.

Was it worth risking his life for five hundred dollars of other people's money? Maybe he could plan a raid and bring it off like a military operation in the old days. It'd be a pleasure to give a bunch of theives a taste of their own medicine.

I'll talk it over with Taggart.

The trail angled downward toward the lake. Stone stopped at the bottom, dismounted, and watered his horse. Then he rolled a cigarette and lit it, looking back toward the wagon train and the mountain range in the distance. The frontier was a living hell because of outlaws like Owsley.

The wagons rumbled toward the lake, circled around, and formed a circle. Stone removed the saddle from his horse and threw it down next to Taggart's wagon. He pulled his spyglass out of his saddlebag and walked up the incline, focusing on the mountains.

That's where Owsley and his men were, not more than five or six miles away. Stone could ride there at night, pick up Owsley's trail, find the hideout, and take back the money while they were asleep.

The crackle of fires and the clanging of pots and pans came to Stone's ears. He walked to Taggart's wagon and sat on the ground. "I want to ride back and get that money."

Taggart chuckled. "Figgered you been thinkin' about that money. So've I. Hate to see a bunch of damn crooks get away with a boodle that size. Reckon you'll need somebody with you, to cover yer back."

"Wouldn't mind some help."

"I'll call a meetin' after supper to talk it over."

They ate beans and biscuits; there was no more fresh meat. After dinner, Stone rounded up the travelers and brought them to Taggart's wagon. The travelers gathered around the campfire, and their faces were drawn and haggard over the loss of money.

"Captain Stone and I've decided to go back and git yer money back," Taggart told them. "It won't be easy, but we know you'll need every cent for when you git to Texas. You just sit tight here and wait for us. Post yer guards and keep yer eyes open. We'll move out after dark. Mister Fenwick will be in charge till we git back."

"What if you don't get back?" Fenwick asked.

"If we don't git back, you'll have to go to Texas without us, but we'll be back. It'll take more'n a bunch of outlaws to stop two old soldiers like me and Captain Stone."

8

NIGHT CAME TO the plains. A full moon shone in the sky, and stars sparkled everywhere. Stone and Taggart rode across the grass, their hats low over their eyes, heading for the mountain range in the distance.

It wasn't hard to find Owsley's trail, because the outlaw hadn't bothered to cover it up. Owsley had ridden right in the middle of the wagon train trail, and it was easy to see his hoofprints going the other way. Every few hundred yards, Stone or Taggart climbed down from their horses to make sure they were still on Owsley's trail.

They didn't talk much. Stone was glad Taggart had come along. Two men were always better than one.

They drew close to the mountain, dismounted, and walked along the trail, pulling their horses by the reins as they studied Owsley's tracks. Stone thought of Owsley's bearded face and tobacco-stained lips. He wanted to see the expression on Owsley's face when he and Taggart took the money back.

"Here it is," said Taggart.

Stone looked at where Taggart was pointing. A set of hoofprints veered to the left, heading for the higher elevations. Stone and Taggart mounted up and followed the tracks. They found themselves on a narrow defile that wound through the foothills and led to the heights.

Stone figured Owsley and his gang never stayed in one spot long, because sooner or later a posse or the cavalry would come after him. He'd hold up a few wagon trains at one pass, then find another pass and hold up other wagon trains there. Probably he was ranging over a wide area, robbing travelers with impunity, always staying on the move so the law couldn't pin him down.

They were moving higher onto the mountain, and Stone thought they were getting close to Owsley's hideout.

"Think we'd better dismount," he said to Taggart.

They climbed down from their horses and led them into the thick brush where they couldn't be seen from the trail. Stone and Taggart tethered the horses to saplings but didn't loosen the cinch straps on the saddles because they might need to mount the horses in a hurry.

They took their rifles and moved back to the trail, following Owsley's tracks on foot. The trail inclined past huge boulders and tall trees, and the breeze rustled the leaves. Then the trail became rocky, and it was difficult to see Owsley's tracks. Stone and Taggart got lost, and it took a half hour before they picked up the tracks again. Stone kept glancing behind him so he could see how the backtrail appeared from the opposite direction. They'd have to return this way, and it was important to keep major landmarks in mind.

It reminded Stone of a night in '63 when he and some of his men from the old Troop C blew up a Yankee ammunition dump in Virginia. They'd sneaked up on it at night just like this, killed the guards, and set fire to the dump. When it blew, it was like an earthquake. The sky filled with fire and the ground had shaken violently.

It had been a successful operation. Stone and his men had felt great afterward, as though they'd accomplished something significant, but it hadn't made any difference. The factories of the North continued to manufacture ammunition by the ton, and the Union won the war.

A horse whinnied ahead, and Taggart and Stone dropped silently to the ground, pulling out their guns. They turned and looked at each other in the darkness. Owsley's camp was straight ahead.

They got down on their bellies and crawled forward like the two old soldiers that they were, cradling their rifles in their arms. They came to a small clearing and saw men sleeping around a smoldering firepit. The men were wrapped in blankets and looked like immense caterpillars. Some had their hats covering their faces. The horses were in a small corral at the edge of the clearing. Stone counted the men, and they were twelve.

Stone turned to Taggart. "Find Owsley."

They roved silently through the campsite, looking for the outlaw leader, gazing into the faces of the sleeping men. The odor of rancid whisky rose to Stone's nostrils; the outlaws had gone on a bender before falling asleep. Taggart raised his hand and waved to Stone then pointed to the man lying at his feet.

Stone moved silently toward Taggart, stepping over the bodies of sleeping men. Finally he drew near Taggart and looked down. Owsley was sleeping there, lying on his back, snoring, a terrible stench rising from his body.

"You cover the others," Stone said to Taggart.

Taggart nodded, turning around and leveling his rifle at the rest of the outlaws. Stone looked down and pressed the barrel of his rifle against Owsley's nose, bending the nose over to the side. Owsley awakened with a start, saw the rifle, and his eyes opened wide.

"Get your hands out where I can see them," Stone said softly.

Owsley brought his hands out from underneath the blanket and held them in the air. The barrel of Stone's rifle was still pressed against his nose, and an expression of stark terror was in Owsley's eyes.

Other outlaws heard Stone's voice and stirred. Taggart held his rifle on them.

"All right—everybody up!" Taggart said. "Raise your hands in the air, and if any man goes for his gun, he's buzzard bait!"

The outlaws opened their eyes and sat on the ground.

They looked at Stone and Taggart, figured the odds, and reached for their guns.

Taggart pulled the trigger of his rifle and drilled one of the outlaws in the chest. Stone spun around and fired off a quick shot, hitting another outlaw in the arm. Taggart jacked his rifle and hit a third outlaw in the mouth.

Owsley saw his chance and dived at Stone's rifle, but Stone pivoted and whacked Owsley over the head with the barrel. Owsley fell back to the ground, and gunsmoke hovered over the campsite. The surviving outlaws raised their hands in the air.

Stone pointed his rifle at Owsley's head. "If anybody moves, I'll blow off this man's head!"

Owsley had a cut above his left eye, and his lips were white. "Don't move boys!" he called out. "Do what they say!"

Taggart moved his rifle from side to side. "Get over here and line up where I can see you."

The outlaws held their hands in the air and walked to the side of the campsite where Stone and Taggart were.

"Keep 'em high, boys," Taggart said, "and let's not try any funny business, because I love to shoot owlhoots."

The outlaws reached toward the moon. Stone prodded Owsley with his rifle. "Line up with them."

Owsley snarled as he got to his feet and took his position to the right of his men.

"I'll cover them," Stone said to Taggart. "You search them."

Taggart walked down the line of men, patting their clothes. He pulled out a few derringers and knives, but none were carrying real guns. They'd never thought anybody would raid their mountain hideout while they were asleep.

"They're clean," Taggart said.

Stone looked at the outlaws, and they were sullen and angry. He turned to Owsley. "We want our money back."

"You ain't gittin' it."

Stone moved toward Owsley and pushed the barrel of

his rifle into Owsley's mouth. "I said we want our money back."

Perspiration poured off Owsley's forehead. "Okay," he said in a muffled voice, because the barrel of Stone's rifle still was in his mouth.

Stone pulled the barrel out of Owsley's mouth. "Where's the money?"

"I already dealt it to my boys."

"Get it back."

Owsley walked around the campsite, gathering saddlebags, and Stone followed him, pointing his rifle at Owsley's back. Owsley carried the saddlebags back to where Taggart was and dropped them on the ground.

"The money's in the saddlebags," he said.

"Empty everything out on the ground."

Stone kept his rifle aimed at Owsley to make sure he didn't pull a pistol out of somebody's saddlebag, but Owsley knew he was being watched and didn't dare take a chance on getting killed. Every saddlebag contained a smaller bag of money. Oswley poured the money onto a pile on the beaten-down grass, while Taggart kept an eye on the outlaws, holding his rifle on them, ready to fire if any of them attacked or tried to run.

They were tense moments, because the outlaws outnumbered Stone and Taggart, but on the other hand, Stone and Taggart were pointing weapons at them. If the outlaws attacked, they might overpower Stone and Taggart, but many of them would be shot down first.

"Take it easy, boys," Taggart said. "It's only money."

Owsley looked up at Stone. "It's all here."

"Stand over there with the others."

Owsley shuffled into line with the rest of his men, and Stone counted the money. Owsley's total was correct. Stone put the money into one of the empty saddlebags and tossed it over his shoulder. Then he stood and aimed his rifle at the outlaws.

Owsley turned down the corners of his mouth. "You talk big with that rifle in your hands. Wonder how big you'd talk if you didn't have it."

Stone looked at the outlaw and felt deep hatred. "You want a gun?"

"Sure."

"Go get one."

"Huh?"

"You and I'll have it out between us. That's what you want, isn't it?"

"That's what I want," Owsley said.

"Get going."

Owsley couldn't believe his good fortune. He walked across the clearing to get his gunbelt and six-gun, and Taggart spoke out of the corner of his mouth to Stone. "You sure you know what yer doin'?"

"He won't beat me to the draw."

Owsley returned, carrying his gunbelt and six-gun.

"Strap it on," Stone said, "and go real slow."

"I'll go slow as you want," Owsley said.

Owsley strapped on his gunbelt in careful, deliberate movements, while Stone aimed his rifle at him.

"Can I tie my holster to my leg?"

"Tie anything you want."

Owsley tied the holster to his leg and looked up.

"You got to let me put a cartridge in the chamber. Otherwise I won't be able to shoot your ass."

"Point your gun over there and do what you gotta do."

Owsley pivoted to the side and pointed his pistol into the woods, twirling the chamber one click so that a cartridge would be ready to fire. Then he dropped the pistol into his holster.

"I'm ready."

Stone turned to Taggart. "Keep an eye on them. If anybody moves, shoot him."

Taggart nodded. Stone faced Owsley and transferred his rifle to his left hand. The two men looked into each other's eyes, and rage crackled between them. The other outlaws watched, certain Owsley would win. Stone and Owsley spread their legs apart and let their right hands dangle in the air above their six-guns.

Owsley wanted to laugh. The damn fool wanted to draw on him. Some people had no sense at all.

"I'm gonna shoot you in the gut and watch you die," Owsley said.

In a sudden, darting movement, Owsley reached for his gun, but Stone already was firing. At the last moment, Owsley saw that he'd made a serious miscalculation.

Stone's pistol barked angrily, and Owsley went flying backward, a widening red splotch on the front of his shirt. He stumbled drunkenly, spat blood, and collapsed on his back.

Taggart took his eyes off the outlaws for a moment to see who'd won the gunfight, and three of the outlaws charged.

He saw them, swung around, and fired. The outlaws were so close he couldn't miss. He jacked the lever quickly and fired again, while Stone got off two quick shots.

When the smoke cleared, the three outlaws were lying on the ground.

Stone aimed his pistol at the other outlaws. "Anybody else feel froggy?"

"Not me," said one of them.

"Me neither," said another.

Taggart aimed his rifle at the remaining outlaws, and they looked seriously demoralized. Stone walked toward Owsley who lay on the ground gasping and vomiting blood. He wasn't quite dead yet and looked up pleadingly at Stone.

"Kill me," Owsley whispered, blood dribbling from his lips.

Stone aimed his pistol at Owsley's head and pulled the trigger. Then he holstered his pistol and leveled his rifle at the remaining outlaws.

"Get two of their horses," Stone said to Taggart, "and run the rest off."

Taggart made for the corral, as Stone kept his rifle aimed at the outlaws. Their hands still were held high in the air, and they looked scared.

"I thought you boys were supposed to be tough outlaws," Stone said.

Taggart saddled two horses and tethered them to the rails, then opened the gate to the corral and fired his pistol a few times. The unsaddled horses stampeded out and disappeared into the night.

"You ain't gonna leave us out here without horses, are you?" one of the outlaws said to Stone.

"Afraid so."

"We're a hundred miles from the nearest town. What're we supposed to do?"

"You figure it out."

Taggart returned with the two saddled horses. Stone continued to aim his rifle at the outlaws.

"You boys get down on your bellies," Stone said.

"You gonna shoot us?" one of them asked fearfully.

"Do as you're told, and you won't get hurt."

The outlaws dropped to the ground and lay flat, glancing nervously at each other.

"Put your hands behind your heads," Stone told them.

The outlaws grimaced as they stretched and folded their hands behind their heads. Stone and Taggart roved across the campsite, taking all the guns and rifles they could find. Then they climbed onto their horses.

"Go!" Stone shouted.

He spurred his horse, and Taggart spurred his. The horses leapt forward and charged away from the campsite. Their hooves thundered on the ground as they galloped down the mountain trail. Stone turned around in his saddle and saw the outlaws scrambling to their feet, running toward their equipment, and he realized the outlaws probably had guns he and Taggart hadn't found.

"Get down!" he shouted to Taggart.

Stone and Taggart bent low over their saddles, and a fusillade of shots erupted behind them. Bullets whizzed over their heads, but then they turned a corner in the trail, and the outlaws were out of sight behind them.

Stone and Taggart rode hard down the mountain trail, leaning over switchbacks and turnarounds, passing beneath massive stone ledges. Finally they reached the spot where they'd tethered their horses. They reined in the ones they'd stolen, and the stolen horses danced and pranced nervously.

"You picked two good ones," Stone said. "I think we should keep them."

They were far from the outlaws, and there was no need to rush. Dismounting from the stolen horses, they climbed onto the ones that they'd ridden to the mountain. They slipped their rifles into their boots on the saddles and tied the reins of the stolen horses to the pommels.

Taggart looked at Stone. "Why'd you draw on Owsley?"

"I didn't like him."

They rode down the mountain and headed across the plain. The moon was low on the horizon and stars twinkled overhead. Stone reached down and patted the saddlebag full of money.

He remembered the first man he'd ever killed. It had been at Manassas, his first combat engagement. The Yankee soldier, on foot, had fired his pistol at Stone and missed, and Stone cut him down with his saber.

It had only taken a few seconds, but Stone never forgot it. It had been like chopping into a thicket of branches—that's what a man's ribs were like. He recalled how the Yankee soldier's eyes had rolled into his head, how blood gushed out of the wound. Stone had been horrified, but he kept charging. He killed more Yankees that day and after a while became cold-blooded and methodical, a professional soldier in every way, fighting for Jeff Davis, Bobby Lee, and the glory of the South.

He and Taggart rode silently across the prairie. In the distance, a wild dog barked, and the stolen horses plodded along dutifully, as if they knew they were stolen and were wondering what their new lives would be like. Stone saw a dark smudge ahead on the prairie, the wagon train.

"We sure showed them outlaws a thing or two," Taggart said. "Next town we come to, I'll tell the sheriff that we wiped out half the Owsley Gang. There might even be a reward."

"We won't be able to collect it, because we haven't brought back any bodies."

Taggart snapped his finger and frowned. "That's right, too. Son of a bitch. We shoulda thought of that."

"We might not've got out of there if we'd taken the time to load on some bodies," Stone told him.

"Sure we coulda," Taggart replied. "We was hot back there, my boy. We coulda done anythin' we wanted."

The wagon train loomed ahead, and Stone saw figures among the wagons. He and Taggart rode closer, and the travelers were hiding behind the wagons, holding their rifles in their hands, ready for the worst.

"It's us!" shouted Taggart. "Don't shoot!"

The travelers surged forward, women and children among them.

"Didja get the money?" Georgie Saulnier asked.

"We got it," Taggart replied.

The travelers raised their arms and cheered. They circled around Stone and Taggart as they rode into the center of the encampment and dismounted. Some of the men slapped them on their backs and shook their hands. The children danced about and clapped their hands. Stone threw the saddlebag full of money onto the ground.

The travelers descended on the saddlebag and poured out the contents. The gold coins glittered in the light of the moon.

"You got back fast," Georgie Saulnier said. "Guess the outlaws didn't put up much of a fight."

The travelers counted the money, and Stone removed the saddle from his horse. He led the horse onto the prairie and rubbed it down with dry grass as the travelers laughed and sang in the distance.

9

THE INCIDENT WITH the Owsley gang drew the travelers closer together. It had been a shared adventure, and all came out better than they'd expected.

People spoke with each other who'd never spoken before. They cooperated and helped more than ever. Barriers of mutual distrust broke down. The travelers became a big family.

The wagon train rolled westward, and the next major stop was Clearfield. The travelers hadn't seen civilization since they'd left Kansas, and everybody dreamed about the big town. They were scheduled to spend three days there.

Stone's horse plodded along steadily, and the steady rocking back and forth and the bright sun produced an hypnotic effect on him. Sometimes he heard snatches of music. Once he thought he heard Marie's voice calling out to him. When he realized he was drifting, he'd snap himself into alertness. The wagon train was relying on him, and he couldn't let them down.

One day he saw a town in the distance and knew it had to be Clearfield. He rode back to the lead wagon, and Taggart sat on the front seat, a cigar sticking out of the corner of his mouth, his knees spread wide apart and his reins held tightly in his hands.

"Clearfield's straight ahead!" Stone told him.

"Figured we'd be a-runnin' into it purty soon."

Stone turned his horse around and rode alongside Taggart's wagon. He didn't want to get his hopes up, but maybe Marie was in Clearfield.

They drew closer to a jumble of buildings in the middle of a fertile valley and camped beside a river on the outskirts of town. Another wagon train was camped on the same river several hundred yards away. They unharnessed their team horses, watered them, and set them to graze.

"One of us should always stay with the wagon train," Taggart said to Stone. "I'll go into town fer supplies now, and then you can go in tonight."

Taggart saddled up one of his riding horses while Stone checked Taggart's wagon to make sure no bolts had worked loose. Taggart and a large group of travelers left for town, leaving only a few at the campsite.

Stone built a fire, boiled some water, and shaved, then bathed in the river. He didn't have any clean shirts left, so he washed one and hung it to dry. He made a pot of coffee for himself and rolled a cigarette.

The tension of the trail gradually left him. There were no marauding tribes of Indians near Clearfield, and he didn't have to worry anymore. The wagon train had been a constant strain. You never knew when danger would strike suddenly.

He sat on the grass with his back against a wagon wheel and watched the other travelers puttering around their wagons. It was a lazy, sunny afternoon. Stone stubbed out his cigarette and closed his eyes for a few moments. Soon he was fast asleep.

He was awakened sometime later by hoofbeats. It was Taggart, sitting atop his horse, looking down at him.

"That's a helluva way to guard the wagon train!"

"Guess I dropped off."

"Guess you did." Taggart looked around and stretched. "No harm done. No Injuns around here."

Taggart took down his bulging saddlebags and carried them to the wagon. "Left my big order at the store," he said. "Pick it up tomorrow." Placing the saddlebags on the ground, he opened a flap and pulled out a bottle of whisky. "This is for the trail."

"Is there a good restaurant in town?"

"Miss Molly Nickerson's. Tell her yer a friend of mine. You can go in now, if you want."

Stone took out a mirror and combed his hair. He thought his face had become leaner since leaving Crawford, and his complexion had turned a deep bronze from the sun. He had a red neck.

He dropped his saddle onto his horse and tightened the cinch. Then he climbed on board, guiding it toward the campfire where Taggart was sitting.

"Don't know when I'll be back," Stone said.

"I'll be here. Watch yer step."

Stone rode toward Clearfield, anticipating a good meal and some good whisky. He wondered if the cowboys from the Rafter K roved this far south. As he drew closer, he could see that Clearfield was larger and much more prosperous than Crawford.

He came to the main street of town, and it was lined with two-story wooden buildings in good repair. There was a hotel, a bank, and a number of saloons. Stone tied up at the first one he saw, and the sign above the door said:

CRYSTAL BALLROOM

Stone jumped onto the boardwalk and paused to let a lady with a bustle in her skirt walk past. Then he approached the swinging front doors of the saloon, pushed his hat to the back of his head, and stepped inside.

The first thing he saw was a big chandelier in the middle of the room, light playing off the many facets of the tiny crystals. Underneath the chandelier were tables, and men of every description sat at them. Some looked like ranchers, others like bums, a few like wealthy town businessmen, and there was the usual, nondescript crowd of cowboys and roughnecks.

They played cards, drank, held conversations. Two wait-

resses carried bottles to tables and cleared away the emp-
ties. The bar was against the far wall opposite the swinging
doors, and Stone headed toward it, weaving among the
tables, looking at the fanned cards in the hands of the
gamblers. He thought he might play a game or two of
cards later if he was still in the mood. There was nothing
quite like a hot game of poker with stakes worth worrying
about.

Finally he came to the bar. It was three deep with men
guzzling whisky and talking in loud tones, gesticulating
vigorously. Stone made his way through them and found
a few inches of open bar. He thrust his arm through it in
an effort to catch the barmaid's eye.

"Whisky," he said.

Plucking down a bottle and a glass, she placed the glass
in front of him and filled it half full of whisky, then told
him how much it cost. She was a blonde in a low-cut gown
and looked as though she wasn't getting much sleep.

She looked Stone up and down and took his money.
She was taller and huskier than Marie, and Stone flashed
on an image of Marie working behind a bar in a frontier
saloon.

Marie had been a rich man's daughter and never had
done any work in her life. Her father gave her anything
she wanted. Work would be a shock, but she'd survive,
because underneath the satin and lace, she'd been tough
and smart.

Something brushed his leg, and he looked to the floor.
It was a big fat black pussycat nudging against him. Stone
picked it up and put it on the bar, scratching in back of
the cat's ears, and the cat raised its head to let him do it.
Static electricity from the cat's fur crackled in Stone's hand.
He raised his glass and took another swig of whisky.

"First time I ever seen him let somebody do that," said
the barmaid. "Who are you, anyway?"

"My name's John Stone."

"I'm Amy."

They looked at each other, then somebody shouted,

"Whisky!" and Amy walked toward the other end of the bar.

Stone petted the cat. "I forgot to find out your name," he said to it.

The man next to him grunted, "You talkin' to cats these days?"

"Guess so," Stone said good-naturedly.

"Any man who talks to a cat must be crazy."

The man was tall and wiry with black hair and a black beard. He wore a dirty yellow shirt and brown cord pants, a six-gun in a holster slung low. Stone turned away and continued to pat the cat.

"Hey—I'm talkin' to you!" the man shouted, grabbing Stone's shoulder. "Don't turn yer goddamn back on me!"

Stone wheeled and faced the man. "I came to this saloon to get a few drinks, and that's all I want it to be."

The man turned down the corners of his mouth in derision. "Is that so!"

Stone ignored the man and continued to pat the cat. Amy leaned over the bar. "Relax cowboy," she said to the man in the yellow shirt. "We don't want no trouble in here."

"Relax your ass!" the man growled. "What the hell do I need to relax fer?" He looked up at Stone. "*I don't like you!*"

"Maybe you should go home and sleep it off."

"Sleep what off?"

Stone held out his hand. "My name's John Stone. What's yours?"

The man looked disdainfully at Stone's hand. "What the hell do I wanna shake hands with you fer?"

Stone let his hand fall slowly to the side. Nothing would mollify the man. *Here we go again.*

The drunken man glowered at him, weaving unsteadily from side to side, his lips curled in contempt. "I think you're a no-good lowdown son of a whore!"

Amy reached over the bar and grabbed the man's shoulder. "Settle down, cowboy."

"Hands off, bitch!"

The man flung her hand off him, then bared his teeth and charged Stone, rearing back his right hand, preparing to deliver a knockout blow, but he was too drunk and too slow. Stone threw a fast left jab that mashed the man's nose and stopped him in his tracks.

The man blinked his eyes. He touched his hand to his nose and blood dripped from his fingers. Drinkers in the vicinity stepped out of the way. The cat jumped to the floor behind the bar.

"You son of a bitch!" the man shouted and raised his hands. "I'm gonna kick your ass!"

Stone gazed wearily at the man and leaned against the bar, not bothering to raise his fists. The man roared and charged, throwing a punch at Stone's head. Stone dodged to the side and hooked a hard left into the man's stomach.

The man's eyes goggled and his tongue stuck out. Doubling up, he keeled over, falling in a clump to the floor where he gurgled and groaned at Stone's feet. Then he began to vomit.

Stone tossed a few coins on the bar and walked toward the door. Outside, he rolled a cigarette and crossed the street, heading for the sheriff's office.

He pushed open the door and stepped inside. A stout man with a badge on his shirt sat at a desk in front of an American flag. He wore a tan suede vest and was cleaning a six-gun.

"What kin I do fer you?" the man asked.

"You the sheriff?"

"I'm Deputy Jones. The sheriff is off tonight."

Stone took out his picture of Marie. "Ever see this woman?"

Deputy Jones looked at it. "Can't say that I have. Who is she?"

"Friend of mine."

"What's she done?"

"She hasn't done anything. Where's Miss Molly Nickerson's restaurant?"

"To the left on the other side of the street."

Stone walked out of the sheriff's office and stopped to

let two riders pass, then he crossed the muddy street. On the far side, sitting on a bench, were Wayne Collins, Joe Doakes, and Georgie Saulnier, the three miners.

"Howdy, boys," Stone said.

Stone passed them by, wondered what they were talking about, and surmised it wasn't anything good. They were the three sleaziest characters on the wagon train. Farther down the block, he saw Stewart and Martha Donahue with their oldest son, Cornelius. Stone touched his finger to the brim of his hat as he passed them, then somebody fired a gun across the street, and Stone reflexively dropped to his belly on the boardwalk.

A drunken cowboy was on the other side of the street, shooting his six-gun into the air. Stone got up and dusted himself off. He saw the big sign straight ahead:

NICKERSON'S RESTAURANT

The front of the restaurant had white gables and a white door. He stepped inside and saw white wallpaper with a pink *fleur de lis* design on it. Men and women sat at the tables, shoveling food into their mouths.

Stone hung his hat on a peg and sat at a table against the wall. Tobacco smoke was thick in the air, and a man on the other side of the room laughed heartily. Stone was looking forward to a peaceful meal, then he'd return to the saloon for a few more drinks, maybe even a card game.

The waitress brought a menu and Stone looked it over. Roast chicken was listed, and he couldn't remember the last time he'd eaten a chicken. The waitress returned to the table, and he told her that's what he wanted.

Stone smoked a cigarette. It felt good to be back in civilization. It reminded him of the days when he went to dinner parties in stately mansions with refined gentlemen and gracious ladies.

A woman in an orange gown entered the dining room via the kitchen door, and Stone assumed she was Miss Molly Nickerson. Her long auburn hair was piled on her head, and she was in her thirties. She flitted from table to table, talking with her customers, and laughter followed wherever she went. Her earrings flashed in the light that streamed through the windows. Finally she reached Stone's table, pulled out a chair, and sat down.

"Who might you be?" she asked.

"John Stone."

"I'm Molly Nickerson. This is my place. You Taggart's scout?"

"Yes, ma'am."

"He told me about you. Said you were a crazy son of a bitch." She narrowed her eyes and looked him over. "Not a bad lookin' feller, either. He said yer lookin' for yer great lost love."

Stone took the picture of Marie out of his pocket. "Ever see her?"

"Oh, she's pretty," said Molly, looking at the photograph. "Looks like a nice girl, but I'm sorry to say I don't think our trails have ever crossed."

She handed the picture back, and he tucked it into his pocket.

"What if you never find her?" Molly asked.

"I'll find her."

"How do you know?"

"I don't know."

"Taggart said yer the fastest gun he ever seen. I could use a man who's fast with a gun, and who's got some grit. You wouldn't be interested in a regular job, would you?"

"Doing what?"

"Workin' for me, helpin' me handle the customers. If there's any trouble, you take care of it. I'll pay you more'n Taggart's payin' you, and I know what he's payin' you: not much. You'll get room and board, too. If yer as smart as I think you are, you'll take the job."

"I thought you and Taggart were friends."

"We are friends, but I need a good man to help me out."

"Should be a lot of good men passing through here."

"I need someone who's smart, honest, good-looking, and hell with a Colt. That combination ain't easy to find."

"I'm on my way to Texas."

"Ain't nothin' in Texas 'cept Injuns and cows. You could make a good livin' here, build up yer stake in case you want to buy a place of yer own someday."

She took a silver cigarette case out of her purse and removed a cigarette that already had been rolled. Placing the cigarette in her mouth, she leaned across the table so Stone could light it with a match.

Her gown was low-cut, and Stone saw the tops of her opulent breasts. Stone figured there'd be more to the job than what she said. He could probably sleep in her bed, too, if he wanted.

"Let me tell you something, John Stone," she said. "I just made you an offer that any other man in this room would've jumped on like a dog jumps on a bone."

"I'm going to Texas."

She blew smoke into the air. "Yer the customer, and the customer is always right. Where's yer dinner?"

"Damned if I know."

"Should've been here by now. I'll check on it. If you change yer mind about the job, you know where to find me."

Molly Nickerson walked toward the kitchen, shaking her rear end from side to side. Stone realized what he'd just given up. No more riding through Indian-infested country for low wages and sleeping on the ground at night. *I could be living in luxury.*

But if he worked for Molly Nickerson, he'd have to toe the mark. She wasn't the kind of woman who fooled around. If she paid him, she'd think she owned him.

His waitress appeared through the smoke, carrying a dish covered with half a chicken.

"Anything else?"

"Whisky."

The waitress receded into the smoke. Stone sliced into the chicken, and it was like cutting through butter. He placed a piece of chicken into his mouth and realized Molly had a first class cook in the kitchen. *I could eat like this all the time.*

Stone knew what it was like to eat well all the time. His family had owned slaves who'd turned out fabulous meals three times a day. He'd been horrified by the food at West Point, but it was eat it or starve. Trail food was trail food, not bad if you wanted roast meat or bacon and beans all the time.

A bulky, squarish figure came toward him through the jumbled tables. It was Taggart, his hat in hand and a grin on his face.

"Reverend McGhee and Fenwick said they'd watch the wagons, so I come back to town for more of Miss Molly's grub. Figured you'd be here by now." Taggart sat at the table and looked at the chicken on Stone's plate. "Think I'll order me that."

At that moment there was a shriek on the other side of the room. "Taggart, you old varmint!" cried Molly Nickerson.

Taggart stood up and she ran into his arms. Everybody looked at the commotion. Taggart patted her ass.

"You meet my scout yet?" he asked.

"Offered him a job, but he wouldn't take it."

Taggart looked at Stone. "I'm touched by yer loyalty to the wagon train, my boy."

"He don't care about yer damn wagon train," she said. "He's thinks that girl in the picture might be in Texas."

"You mean," Taggart said to Stone, "if it wasn't for that woman in yer pocket, you would've left me?"

"It was an awfully handsome offer."

"You'd just leave me stranded here in the middle of nowhere?"

"The town is full of men who'd be happy to work for you."

"Nobody's loyal anymore." Taggart shook his head sadly.

A waitress scurried up to Miss Molly Nickerson and whispered in her ear.

"Excuse me," Molly said.

She rose from the table and headed toward the kitchen.

Stone guessed they were running out of something, or maybe the stove had broken down.

Taggart filled his glass with whisky. "Actually, if it was me, to be perfectly honest with you, I would've accepted her offer. I once had a woman who took care of me for a while, and it was real nice. 'Course, that was a long time ago."

"Who was she?"

"A sportin' lady. It was back in San Francisco, when I used to play cards for a livin'."

"You were a gambler, Taggart?"

"For a time."

"You must've been hell in those days."

"Still am." Taggart sipped some whisky. "You know, Miss Molly don't offer jobs to people every day."

"You trying to get rid of me?"

"No, but she don't hire just anybody. I've knowed her for a long time, and she's only had a few men here."

"What happened to them?"

"She throwed 'em all out after a while."

"She'd probably throw me out after a while, too."

"Prob'ly."

The waitress brought Taggart's chicken, and he cut open the breast and, placing a piece into his mouth, chewed like a cow.

"By the way," he said, his mouth full, "the first place I went looking for you was the saloon, and they was talkin' about a fight they had in there. The feller who won fit yer description. Was it you?"

"Wasn't much of a fight."

"The feller you punched is from the Circle Y, and his buddies're mad. They're probably gonna be a-lookin' fer you, so be careful. You'd better stay outta that saloon, but I guess the first thing you'll do after leavin' here is go back there."

"That's what I'd intended. Haven't spent much time in saloons lately."

"Don't look for trouble, boy. Someday you'll meet somebody faster'n you."

"A man's got a right to take a drink if he wants to. You don't have to come if you don't want to."

"Somebody's got to watch yer back, you damn fool."

They ate heartily, and the chickens before them were picked clean to the bones. For dessert they had large wedges of apple pie and hot black coffee. Stone rolled a cigarette and Taggart lit a cigar. Miss Molly walked toward them, sitting at their table, crossing her legs.

"Change yer mind?" she said to Stone.

"No, ma'am."

"I could've used you." She turned to Taggart. "How about you?"

"Can't leave my wagon train."

She raised her eyebrows. "Why the hell not? You think them people give a damn about you? If they find somebody who'll move 'em cheaper, they'll run in a minute."

"I won't be workin' wagon trains much longer," Taggart said. "I want to settle down on my ranch in Texas. Don't think my woman would appreciate me workin' here for you, Miss Molly."

She leaned toward Taggart and put her arm around his shoulders, pressing her breasts into his arm and kissing him on the cheek. Then she looked at Stone. "I can understand Taggart's reason," she said, "because he's got somethin' in Texas a-waitin' for him, but you ain't got nothin' a-waitin' for you, John Stone. Let me tell you somethin': Life is like a dogsled. If yer not the lead dog, the scenery never changes. I'm a-givin' you a chance to be the lead dog, but you ain't smart enough to take it."

"Maybe I'll come back to you someday," Stone said.

"You don't take it now, you ain't gittin' it, ever."

"Got to go to Texas."

"Why is it the good men don't want me, and the bad ones're comin' out of the woodwork?" She looked around her noisy restaurant, and a customer was arguing with a waitress. "Got to git back to work."

She rose from the table and walked toward the irate customer. Taggart puffed his cigar. "Can't figger you out," he said to Stone. "Sometimes I think yer smart and sometimes I think yer dumb."

Stone smoked his cigarette and thought of how nice it would be to sleep in a clean bed every night, but Marie was out there someplace, and he had to find her.

"Let's hit that saloon," he said to Taggart.

"Not only are you dumb, but yer loco to boot. I'm tellin' you, the boys from the Circle Y are liable to be there, and that'll spell trouble in anybody's book."

"You don't have to come if you don't want to."

"I'm comin'," Taggart said. "Yer like a little kid—can't leave you alone or you'll git into trouble."

They paid their check and headed for the door. Miss Molly Nickerson sashayed toward them, kissed Taggart's cheek, then held out her hand to Stone.

"Nice meeting you," she said. "Just remember what I told you about that dogsled."

Taggart opened the door, and they stepped outside into the cool night breeze. Stone looked down the street and saw the bright lights of the saloon illuminating crowds of men on the boardwalk drinking whisky out of bottles.

"Don't like the look of it," Taggart said.

"I've been on the trail for nearly three weeks," Stone replied. "I feel like relaxing in a saloon, and that's what I'm gonna do."

They walked down the street toward the saloon, passing stores closed for the night and drunks sprawled on benches, empty bottles of whisky in their hands. As they drew closer to the saloon, one of the cowboys looked at them.

"There he is!"

He pointed at Stone and Taggart, and others looked in their direction.

"Let's git 'em!" the cowboy said.

They spilled off the boardwalk onto the street, heading toward Stone and Taggart, and they were burly, mean-looking men wearing jeans and carrying guns.

"Hope yer satisfied," Taggart said.

Stone looked at the cowboys approaching on the street and felt anger. He didn't go through five years of war to be told he couldn't go to a saloon for a drink. There were seven cowboys, and they crowded onto the boardwalk, blocking the way.

"We're from the Circle Y!" the one in front said. His hat was low over his eyes, and he had frizzy blond sideburns. "You better get the fuck out of town."

"Make me," Stone said.

The cowboys looked at each other, grinned, raised their fists, and rushed toward Stone and Taggart, who lowered their heads and charged. They collided with the cowboys in the middle of the walkway, and fists flew through the air.

Stone ducked a punch, whacked a cowboy in the gut, and found himself standing in front of the blond cowboy with long frizzy sideburns. The blond cowboy threw a long, loping overhand left cross, and Stone blocked it easily. He stepped forward and rammed the blond cowboy in the mouth with his elbow. The blond cowboy's teeth were knocked down his throat, and his lips were pulped. Stone took a step to the side and threw a sharp right hook. He connected with the cowboy's temple, and the cowboy dropped like a hunk of lead.

Another cowboy jumped onto Stone's back, wrapping his arm around Stone's throat. Stone bent forward and jabbed his elbow into the cowboy's stomach, then spun around, throwing the cowboy off him. Stone shot an uppercut to the cowboy's chin, and it straightened him up and sent him flying through the air. Stone didn't have time to see where he landed, because three other cowboys dived on him from front and behind, causing him to lose his balance, and he fell to the ground.

The cowboys dropped on top of him, punching and kicking, and Stone punched and kicked back. He rolled around on the ground with the three cowboys, and they became buried in a cloud of dust, arms and legs flailing, grunting and hollering. One of the cowboys tried to gouge out Stone's eyes with his thumbs, but Stone grabbed the thumbs with his hands and bent them back until they cracked. The cowboy screamed and pulled away from the pack.

Another cowboy punched Stone in the mouth, but Stone grasped the cowboy by the throat and hurled him away. One of the cowboys standing tried to kick Stone in the head, and the pointy toe of the cowboy's boot struck Stone on the right temple, opening a cut.

Stone roared like a lion and jumped to his feet. He saw Taggart lying on his back in the middle of the boardwalk, out cold, and four cowboys from the Circle Y advanced toward Stone.

"Get 'im, boys," one of them said.

They charged in unison, and Stone kicked one of them in the chest, knocking the wind out of him. He punched another in the nose, flattening it like a pancake. The third cowboy punched Stone hard on the chin, but Stone counterpunched quickly with a left-right combination that sent the man reeling to the ground.

One cowboy remained on his feet, and he looked around uncertainly. He was an inch or two shorter than Stone, but wider in the waist.

"C'mon," Stone said.

The cowboy had a round head and a grim smile on his face. He raised his fists and stepped forward, and Stone jabbed him quickly in the forehead, between his raised hands. The blow didn't budge the heavyset cowboy, although Stone's knuckles split the skin on the cowboy's forehead, and a trickle of blood dropped down into his eyebrows. The cowboy feinted a left, which Stone blocked, and then the cowboy drove a right into Stone's midsection, but it was like hitting a wall.

Stone stepped forward, and so did the cowboy. They threw punches at all angles at each other, some connecting, some missing. Stone took as much as he gave, and the crowd in front of the saloon watched noisily, cheering them on, wondering which one would fall first.

Stone tasted blood in his mouth, and spat it onto the ground. He and the cowboy circled each other then rushed at each other again. They came together in the middle of the street, hurling punches. Stone kept hitting the cowboy in the face, but the cowboy wouldn't go down, and the cowboy managed to land a stunning punch to Stone's forehead.

Stone decided he'd better concentrate on his defense. He stepped back, blocked a few punches, dodged a few others, and looked for openings. Whenever he saw one, he shot a hard punch through. The cowboy was a rough-and-tumble fighter but didn't know much about boxing. Stone picked him apart with jabs, hooks, and uppercuts. Soon the cowboy's face was a mask of blood, and he wheezed through his swollen lips. Getting tired, he lowered his left hand. Stone saw the opening and launched a measured right hook over the low left hand and connected with the cowboy's cheek. The cowboy blinked and took a step backward. Stone went after him, throwing crunching lefts and rights. The cowboy sagged to the left and then to the right. Stone loaded up on another right hook and struck the cowboy on the ear. The cowboy's knees gave way, and he collapsed to the ground.

Stone took a deep breath and looked around. All the cowboys from the Circle Y were lying on the ground. Stone bent over and picked up his hat, placing it squarely on his head. Then he walked toward Taggart sprawled in the middle of the walkway.

"What happened?" Taggart asked.

Stone helped Taggart rise to his feet, and Taggart looked at the men from the Circle Y lying on the boardwalk and in the street.

"We really kicked the shit out of 'em, didn't we, boy?"

"I'll drink to that!" Stone replied.

Together they walked toward the front door of the saloon. Townspeople stared at them, pointing and talking excitedly, while the cowboys from the Circle Y picked themselves off the ground and staggered toward their horses, their arms around each other's shoulders, trying to hold each other up, wondering what hit them.

Stone and Taggart walked side by side toward the bar, and Amy still was on duty.

"Whisky," Stone said.

"You fellers look like you been in a fracas."

Taggart placed his belly against the bar. "We just stomped the boys from the Circle Y."

She poured two glasses of whisky, and they raised them to their lips, gulping down every last drop. Then she filled the glasses again.

"Goddamn!" Taggart said, his left eye turning black. "I feel like a kid again! We ought to do that more often!"

10

STONE WOKE UP feeling as if a stagecoach had run over him. He smelled coffee and bacon, and opened his eyes. Taggart squatted beside the fire, throwing a few more sticks on. "Mornin'," said Taggart, his left eye a greenish shade of purple. "How're you feelin'?"

"Terrible."

Stone rolled away from his blankets and picked up his tin cup. He made his way to the fire and sat heavily beside Taggart. Taggart poured coffee into the cup, and Stone sipped the hot liquid. He looked around the campsite, and many of the other travelers also were awake, making breakfast, working on their wagons.

Then Stone heard a commotion on the other side of the campsite. It was Jason Fenwick screaming: "I've been robbed!"

Fenwick ran toward Stone and Taggart, waving his arms in the air, hollering desperately. He was followed by his wife, their two sons, and two daughters. Everyone looked at them, and Taggart got to his feet.

"My money's gone!" Fenwick shouted.

"Maybe you'd better sit down," Taggart said.

Fenwick was too agitated to sit down. "I just checked to see if my money still was safe, and somebody took every penny of it! I'm ruined!"

"Where was the money?" Taggart asked.

"Beneath the floorboards of my wagon. Somebody pried them up, took the money, and returned the floorboards to where they was."

"How much did they get?"

"Six thousand dollars!"

Taggart said to Stone, "We'd better go take a look."

They followed the Fenwicks to their wagon, and Stone was struggling with a massive headache. He and Taggart had drunk whisky until they could barely stand, and Stone had no idea how he'd returned to the campsite.

They came to the Fenwick wagon, and the tailgate had been let down. The floorboards were removed, revealing a false bottom. "That's where the money was," Fenwick said. "Now it's gone."

Stone wasn't in very good condition, but he could feel the immensity of the tragedy. Fenwick had been a rich man, relative to the others on the wagon train, and now he was the poorest. He had a wife and family and was in the middle of the great plains without a dime to his name.

"I don't know what to do," Fenwick said to Taggart, wringing his hands. "Nothing like this has ever happened to me before."

A crowd had gathered. Reverend McGhee placed his arm around Fenwick's shoulders, and Fenwick looked as though he was going to cry.

Taggart said to Stone, "See if anybody's missin'."

Stone looked at the people in the crowd, checking off each face, but some faces weren't there. He sauntered to the wagon owned by the two gamblers, Tad Holton and Sam Drake, and heard snores emanating from within. Stone looked over the tailgate and saw two figures lying on the floorboards, covered with blankets. Stone pulled the blankets away and saw Holton and Drake sleeping like babies, their mouths open, stinking of whisky.

Next Stone made his way to the wagon owned by Mike Leary, Frank Maxsell, Homer Hodge, and Lou Tramm, the dudes from the East. He saw three of them sprawled around their wagon, their heads covered with blankets, and one lying in the back of the wagon. Stone pulled down their blankets so he could see their faces, and all four were there. They too smelled strongly of whisky.

Stone headed for the miners' wagon and couldn't see anyone sleeping on the ground around the wagon. He looked in the back, and no one was inside. They hadn't been in the crowd that'd comforted the Fenwicks. Where the hell were they?

Stone walked toward the remuda. He examined the horses, and the ones belonging to the miners were gone. Stone returned to the miners' wagon and looked for their saddles but couldn't find them. Their frying pan and coffee pot were missing also, along with some of their clothes.

Stone returned to the Fenwick wagon. Mary Fenwick lay on the ground in a dead faint, and the other women were attending to her. Jason Fenwick paced back and forth, muttering to himself that he was ruined, and Taggart patted him on the shoulder, trying to comfort him.

"I know it's a bad break," Taggart said, "but you'll have to keep goin'. Maybe you can get a job, or maybe you can borry some money from a bank."

Stone approached them. "The miners are missing. Their horses are gone and so are their saddles, cooking gear, and clothes."

Jason Fenwick jumped into the air. "I knew it was them! They was always hangin' around my wagon, actin' suspicious! Remember I told you somebody'd been in my wagon? It must've been them! I'd better go into town right now and tell the sheriff!"

Taggart spat into the grass. "The sheriff ain't gonna do nothin'."

"He's got to go after them crooks! They got all my money! Somebody's got to do somethin'!"

"He won't do nothin' unless it happens right underneath his nose."

Jason Fenwick sputtered impotently, balling up his fists.

Stone hitched his thumbs in his gunbelts. "They couldn't've gone far," he said, "and they're not exactly mountain men. Maybe I can pick up their trail."

Jason Fenwick's face brightened. "Would you go after them?" he asked. "I'll come with you! Maybe we can track them down together."

"I'd rather go alone."

"If you git my money back, I'll make it worth your while."

Taggart said, "Don't git yer hopes up, Mister Fenwick. There's a lot of country out there. It won't be easy to track them boys down."

Fenwick looked at Stone. "I'd appreciate anything you could do."

Stone walked back to Taggart's wagon. He thought of Wayne Collins, Joe Doakes, and Georgie Saulnier, and he'd never liked them. If he were they, what would he do? Head for the nearest town to buy supplies.

He returned to Taggart's wagon, took down his saddle-bags and pulled out his map. Clearfield was the closest town, and the next closest was Rendale to the north.

He heard footsteps and turned around. It was Taggart, alone. "Mighty good of you to go after them miners," Taggart said. "Why you doin' it?"

"Hard to say."

"Which way you think they're headed?"

"Rendale."

Taggart looked at the map. "Makes sense."

Stone filled his saddlebags with canned beans and a hunk of bacon plus coffee and an old lard tin to boil the water in. Then he saddled his horse.

"How long you think you'll be gone?" Taggart asked.

"I'll give it a week, no more."

"We're movin' out in the mornin'. You know our route. Shouldn't be hard for you to catch up with us after yer finished chasin' them damn miners. I'm a-gonna miss you. I'll have to be my own scout from now on."

They shook hands.

"Be careful," Taggart said.

Stone climbed onto his horse. The horse pranced side-ways and backward, and Stone pulled on the reins. He pointed the horse's head toward Rendale, and touched his spurs to its flanks. Stone rode out of the campsite, and the travelers watched him go, wondering if they'd ever see him again.

His horse plodded over the prairie, and Stone thought of the three miners. Some men would rather steal than work, and that didn't set right with him. Fenwick worked hard all his life to save his stake, and nobody had a right to take it away.

Stone saw Clearfield straight ahead and angled his horse to the west. He intended to swing wide around the town and then try to cut the trail left by the miners between Clearfield and Rendale. There'd be lots of tracks, but at one point they should thin out. Stone didn't imagine many people traveled regularly all the way to Rendale.

He rode around Clearfield and continued in a northeasterly direction, passing herds of cattle grazing in the sun. The terrain was gently rolling hills with a few mountains in the distance. He didn't stop for lunch because he knew he had to stay on the trail. He munched biscuits in the saddle and washed them down with water. In the afternoon, he turned east, hoping to cut the miners' trail.

He searched the ground for hoofprints or the lay of grass that indicated that riders had passed, but all he saw was open prairie. Occasionally he came to groups of cattle, and some had the Circle Y brand.

Several times he climbed down from his horse to look at tracks, but they were always the tracks of cattle, and he was looking for horseshoes. Late in the day he came to the tracks of a solitary horseman heading north toward Rendale, but the tracks weren't deep, and it was probably just a lone cowboy working the range.

A half-hour later he came to a substantial number of hoofprints, but the horses weren't shod. He hoped he wouldn't blunder into a Comanche war party. He continued his swing to the east as the sun dropped toward the horizon behind him.

It was lonely, eye-straining work. He came to a mass of buffalo tracks and searched among them for the hoofprints of horses but couldn't find any. Then, farther along, he came to a fresh trail left by at least ten shod horses, which indicated a fairly large party traveling north to Rendale. Could the miners have joined such a party? Stone thought it over and decided the miners probably would be wary of associating with anybody.

Stone continued to move eastward and wondered if he was on a wild goose chase. How could he expect to find three men in such a big country? But horses left tracks. There was the outside chance he could pick up their trail.

He found more cattle tracks and something that looked like the tracks of a bear. In the late afternoon, he came to another trail. Climbing down from his horse, he examined it, and it looked like three shod horses had passed that way. The tracks headed north to Rendale, and Stone thought he'd found the miners.

He climbed onto his horse again and followed the trail. It continued in a northerly direction but then suddenly turned east sharply, and that baffled Stone. He stopped his horse and unfolded his map. The nearest town to the east was almost two hundred miles away. Where had those riders been headed?

Then the answer came to Stone. The riders probably were cowboys headed toward a ranch, because ranches weren't marked on the map. He'd been led astray.

Stone decided that he'd gone far enough to the east. It was time to swing back to the west, but soon it'd be dark. His tactics hadn't paid off.

He wondered if there wasn't a better way. Should he head straight for Rendale and try to beat the miners there? If he rode all night, guiding himself with his compass and the stars, maybe he could do it. The miners probably would sleep that night, unaware anybody was following them.

He checked his map and compass and pointed the horse in a northerly direction. The sun sank lower on the horizon, and the sky turned a brilliant crimson. Then it grew darker and the stars came out. Stone found the North Star and placed it between his horse's ears.

He realized now that he should have made for Rendale immediately after leaving camp instead of trying to cut the miners' trail. That had cost him precious time, but it had seemed a reasonable idea at the time.

Night birds called to each other from the bushes. He passed piles of fresh buffalo dung and crossed an expanse of flat rock. Somewhere out there, the miners were sleeping with their stolen money.

Around midnight he came to a river with grass on both sides. He loosened the cinch strap of the saddle and watered his horse, then let it graze while he opened a can of beans and ate them cold with a spoon.

He was getting tired. Coffee would help, but he didn't have time to brew it. He threw the empty can of beans over his shoulder and drank water out of his canteen. Then he filled the canteen at the riverbank and tied it to the pommel on the saddle. He tightened the cinch strap and climbed onto the horse.

The horse splashed across the river. Stone held his rifle in the air so it wouldn't get wet. The horse climbed up the far side, and Stone urged him onward.

They crossed the high grass and plunged into a forest, gloomy and dark. Stone peered through the murky stillness, looking for unusual movement. His right hand drew one of his pistols, just in case.

He emerged from the forest, and a shooting star streaked across the heavens. The horse trudged onward, jerking its head up and down. Stone drooped in the saddle, and his eyes closed. A few times he awoke with a start after drifting off to sleep for a few moments.

He smoked a cigarette to keep him awake and rode through the night, a lone figure on an endless prairie. It reminded him that during the war he'd stay awake for two or three days, fighting and riding hard. If he could do it then, he could do it now.

The horse trudged across endless vistas of prairie, while the sky pulsated with myriad stars. Stone thought of all the people snug in their beds, safe for the night, while he was chasing thieves. He wondered where Marie was sleeping and hoped she was sleeping alone.

He saw the glimmer of dawn on the horizon. At first he

thought his eyes were playing tricks with him, but then the glimmer grew, and he realized the sun was rising and a new day beginning. He was hungry and bone tired, and his horse needed to rest. He decided to stop for breakfast.

It still was dark when he climbed down from his saddle and set the horse to graze. Dew was heavy on the grass, so the horse would get water, too. Stone ate his last two biscuits plus another can of cold beans. He wished he had time to fry bacon, but he had to beat the thieves to Rendale.

He finished his meal and rolled a cigarette. He thought he should let the horse graze a bit longer, because once he started riding, he didn't intend to stop again until he hit Rendale.

The day became brighter. A few large puffy clouds floated past. He hoped it wouldn't rain. Climbing into the saddle, he prodded the horse toward Rendale.

Then he saw it: a column of smoke rising up from the plains into the sky. Somebody was cooking breakfast. They'd most likely be cowboys, but there weren't any cattle around. It wasn't a heavily-traveled area. Could it be the miners having breakfast? It was a longshot, but it was possible. He thought he'd ride closer, dismount, and sneak up on the people at the fire to see who they were. If they were strangers, he'd back off and continue on his way to Rendale. If they were the miners, he'd have a showdown.

He checked his rifle and pistols. They could be Indians or an outlaw gang. He'd have to approach carefully and not take any chances.

He came to a thicket and dismounted, picketing his horse in a hollow where it couldn't be seen unless someone rode directly inside. He patted the horse on the mane and pulled his rifle out of its boot. Bending low, he moved toward the fire.

It was several hundred yards away through bushes and high grass. Stone kept a low silhouette as he edged forward, pausing occasionally to look and listen. He held his rifle in both hands, ready to aim and fire quickly. He didn't think they were Indians, because Indians wouldn't build a fire in the middle of the plains where the cavalry could attack easily. They were probably white men.

The time had come to get down on his belly and crawl. He dropped to the dirt and crept forward, cradling his rifle in his arms. Inch by inch he advanced toward the campfire, then he heard a peal of laughter that stopped him cold.

It was laughter that had a familiar ring, and Stone recognized it as the voice of Wayne Collins, the miner whose ear he'd shot off. The thieves were heading toward Rendale as he'd thought, and he'd caught up with them. They shouldn't've lit that fire, but evidently thought they were safe.

He crawled closer and heard the voices of the miners more distinctly. They sounded happy, free and clear with six thousand stolen dollars, but they hadn't counted on John Stone.

Stone inched forward and peered through the grass. He could see them gathered around their fire, eating bacon and biscuits and drinking coffee. Stone smelled the aroma and it made his mouth water. Their horses were picketed nearby.

"The first thing I'm gonna do," Georgie Saulnier said, "is find the fattest whore in town. I'm a-gonna strip her down and have me a real good time."

"I'm a-gonna git me a meal in the best restaurant," Collins said. "This damn trail grub is makin' me sick."

"Whisky," said Joe Doakes, scratching his armpit. "I'm a-gonna drink me a whole bottle then go to sleep in a real feather bed."

Stone stood and walked toward them, aiming his rifle at them. "Morning."

They stared at him, eyes bulging out of their heads and then went for their guns. Stone pulled the trigger of his rifle, and Joe Doakes' hand froze in midair, an expression of shock on his face. A red splash appeared on the front of his shirt, and he keeled over. Wayne Collins and Georgie Saulnier dropped their guns and raised their hands slowly into the air.

"Keep 'em high!" Stone said, walking toward them. "Stand up!"

They got to their feet, reaching for the sky. Stone walked behind them, pulled their pistols out of their holsters and stuffed them into his belt. Georgie Saulnier turned around suddenly and lunged for Stone's rifle, but Stone bashed him in the mouth with his rifle butt. Saulnier's derby hat was knocked off his head, and he dropped to the ground.

Stone moved in front of Wayne Collins, who broke into a nervous smile. "Well, howdy, Cap'n. What're you doin' out here?"

"Where's the money?"

"What money?"

Stone aimed his rifle at Wayne Collins' head.

"I said, where's the money!"

"Let's make a deal."

"No deals."

Collins forced a grin. "Yer a little greedy, ain't'cha?"

"Get the money."

"I don't know where it is."

Stone nudged the barrel of his rifle under Wayne Collins' chin. "You'd better remember real fast."

Wayne Collins looked like he'd faint. Georgie Saulnier moaned and opened his eyes. He shook his head and tried to figure out what had happened. Then he saw Stone in front of Collins, the rifle in his hands, and it all came back.

"Get up," Stone said to him.

Georgie dragged himself to his feet and spat blood onto the ground. "What do you want?" he asked, adjusting the derby on his head.

"Keep your hands up."

"Let's make a deal."

Wayne Collins said, "I already tried. He didn't go for it."

Georgie smiled at Stone, showing teeth rinsed with blood. "I always figured you was a crook. You want it all fer yerself, eh? Waal, I guess there ain't nothin' much we can do. Take it."

"Go get it—the both of you—and if you try anything, I'll fill you with lead."

Georgie Saulnier shot a meaningful glance at Wayne Collins, then they walked around the campfire to the other side, where saddles and equipment were piled up on the ground.

"Go real slow," Stone said, "and don't try anything."

"It's in them saddlebags right there," Georgie said.

"Show me, and keep your hands out where I can see them."

Georgie moved toward the pile of equipment. He pulled a worn leather set of saddlebags out of the pile and laid them on the ground. Unfastening the flap, he thrust his hand inside.

"Easy now," Stone said, moving his rifle back and forth between Wayne Collins and Georgie Saulnier.

Georgie pulled his hand out of the saddlebag, and he had a gun in it. The sound of gunshots echoed across the prairie. Georgie's bullet whistled past Stone's right shoulder, but Stone's bullet struck Georgie in the chest. Georgie screamed horribly, clutching his hands to the wound, and Wayne Collins leapt over the fire, wrapping his arms around Stone's waist, trying to throw him to the ground.

Stone didn't throw easily. Wayne Collins grunted and tugged, but Stone was solid as a statue with its foundation buried in the ground. Stone raised his fist in the air and brought it down hard on top of Wayne Collins' head, and the miner loosened his grip, collapsing at Stone's feet.

Stone patted Wayne Collins down to make sure he had no weapons on him and found a knife in his boot. He pulled it out and threw it into the fire. Then he walked toward Georgie Saulnier, who lay on his back, his hands over his chest, blood oozing between his fingers.

"You got me," Georgie Saulnier whispered hoarsely.

Stone reached into the saddlebags and came out with a handful of money. He opened the other side of the saddlebag, and there was money in there, too. Georgie Saulnier coughed, and blood trickled out the corner of his mouth.

"It burns," he whispered.

A few feet away, Wayne Collins got to his hands and

knees. Stone walked over to him and pointed the rifle at his head. "Get up."

"I'm a-gittin'."

Wayne Collins pushed himself to his feet. He staggered to one side and then to the other, his jaw hanging open, blinking his eyes. He looked at Georgie Saulnier, and Georgie wasn't breathing anymore. Georgie's eyes were wide open and staring, and the skin on his hands and arms was waxen.

"I do believe he's daid," Wayne Collins said.

"You're going to be dead, too, if you try another of your tricks."

"What you gonna do with me?"

"Take you back to the law."

"Why don't you keep the money and let me go?"

"Stand over there."

Wayne Collins moved sullenly toward where Stone indicated with the barrel of his rifle. Stone dropped to one knee and looked into the saddlebags. Wayne Collins saw his chance and dived.

Stone brought his rifle around, but wasn't fast enough. Wayne Collins smashed him in the mouth with his fist, then tried to yank the rifle out of Stone's hands. Stone held on tightly, and the two men rolled around on the ground as they struggled for possession of the rifle.

Wayne Collins wasn't able to pull the rifle from Stone's iron grip, so he reached desperately down to Stone's gunbelt, but Stone slammed him in the mouth with the butt of the rifle. The force of the blow threw Wayne Collins onto his back.

Stone stood over him. "Get up."

Wayne Collins held his hand over his busted lips and rose to his feet. "I learned my lesson," he said. "I won't try nothin' again."

"Stand in front of me and turn around."

"What're you gonna do?"

"I'll put a bullet in your head unless you do as I say."

Wayne Collins turned his back to Stone, who picked a length of rope out of the pile of equipment. He tied Collins' hands behind his back, then forced him to his knees and tied his hands to his ankles so he couldn't move.

"You ain't gonna leave me like this, are you, pard?"

"Your pards are dead."

Stone upended the saddlebags on the ground and counted the money, while Wayne Collins writhed on the ground, trying to work his way out of the ropes, but they were too tight. The money amounted to six thousand dollars as Fenwick had said. Stone stuffed it into the saddlebags and slung the saddlebags over his shoulder. Then he strode toward the miners' horses.

Collins' eyes widened like saucers. "Now hold on! You cain't leave me like this!"

Stone lifted one of the miners' saddles and a blanket, carrying them to the best-looking horse of the bunch. He threw the blanket over the horse's back and then put the saddle in place.

"Please!" pleaded Wayne Collins. "You cain't do this to me! I'll die out here! It ain't Christian, what yer doin' to me! I'll give you anythin' I got!"

Stone placed the saddlebags full of money behind the saddle, then filled another saddlebag with canned food and bacon. He threw that saddlebag over the back of another horse.

Wayne Collins screamed hysterically: "You gotta tell me why you're doin' this! I ain't never done nothin' to you! Don't leave me here! The coyotes'll get me! How'd you like to get eaten alive by a damn coyote!"

"You can't be trusted," Stone said.

"That was before!" Wayne Collins hollered, his eyes bulging out of his head. "This is now! Take all the damn money—I never wanted it in the first place! It was all Georgie's idea! I just went along with him! Gimme another chance!"

Stone tied the horses together. He dropped the miners' weapons into a gunny sack and lashed it to the saddle of the third horse. Then he mounted the horse he'd saddled. Wayne Collins looked at him from ground level, his hands and feet tied together behind his back.

"Please don't do this to me! Shoot me—do anything you want to me—*but don't leave me here!*"

Stone touched his spurs to the horse's flanks, and the horse stepped forward, the other two horses following. "No!" Collins screamed as Stone rode away. "Please!" Collins blubbered and cried, tears rolling down his cheeks. The horror of his predicament hit him with full force. "Don't leave me here! I'll do anything you say!"

Stone didn't look back. He continued to ride toward the horse he'd picketed in the hollow.

"Come back!" screamed Wayne Collins, his face streaked with tears. "Don't leave me like this!"

Stone rocked back and forth in his saddle as his horse made its way toward the hollow. Wayne Collins' voice grew fainter behind him. Then it merged with the wind, and Stone wasn't sure which was which anymore.

11

TAGGART SAT ERECTLY in his saddle, scanning the terrain ahead, and saw bald knobs with hogbacks and scattered bushes. Good drygulch country, and he'd been attacked by Comanches in this area in the past. He peered from bush to hill, looking for Indian sign, but his eyes weren't as good as they used to be, and sometimes things got blurred. Especially on a hot day in the bright sun.

He took off his hat, wiped his forehead with the back of his arm, reached for his canteen. The Comanches had swarmed out from behind those hills once and attacked a wagon train he'd been on before it could circle. It had been touch and go during the first five minutes, but Indian arrows and lances were no match for Henry and Sharps rifles.

He drank from the canteen, and the water was warm with a metallic taste. His lower intestines ached from beans. Something hurt in his back. He was too old to ride a horse all day, but Stone was gone, and when would he come back?

He'd been gone two days, and there was no sight of him. Taggart thought maybe he shouldn't't've let him go, but he'd been feeling sorry for Fenwick, and Stone had been determined to get the money back.

Stone was always sticking his neck out, couldn't stay out

of trouble. Taggart had been the same way when he was young. He'd loved kicking the shit out of people, chasing women, and raising hell. Now he wanted to sit on the porch with the wife and watch the cattle grazing in the fields.

He turned around and saw the wagon train meandering through the hills. Wagon trains were for young men full of piss and vinegar, like John Stone. Stone didn't know how to back down and was too confident of his skill with guns. Taggart wondered about the picture of the girl. She'd probably run off with somebody else and didn't have the guts to tell him.

Taggart saw an odd shape in the hills and squinted at it. Was it an Indian on a horse, an ocotillo bush, or an antelope? Twenty years ago, he'd have known, but now his vision was fuzzy.

He wished John Stone would get back, so he could travel on the wagon. His back didn't hurt so much when he was sitting on the front seat of the wagon, and all he'd have to do was hold the ribbons. Stone would know what was out there. Taggart stared at the shape, and it was gone. Taggart felt irritated with himself.

Where the hell is John Stone?

It was night, the sky was cloudy, and Stone couldn't see a damn thing. According to his map, the town of Fairhope was supposed to be dead ahead, but there was only blackness.

He was on an enormous plain, and had been traversing it most of the day, thinking about reaching Fairhope that night and checking into the best hotel in town.

Either the map was wrong or his dead reckoning was off. It was possible he was lost. The North Star was obscured by clouds, and maybe his compass was broken. For all he knew, he was going around in circles.

Might as well camp here. No sense going in the wrong direction. Tomorrow he could start fresh and see where he was headed. He raised his leg and prepared to dismount when something in the distance caught his eye.

It was a dot of light flickering faintly, maybe Fairhope.

Stone decided to keep going. He settled into his saddle and turned to look at the three horses following him. Maybe he could sell them for a good price in Fairhope.

The horses quickened their pace, because they saw the light, too. It was straight ahead, and Stone was directly on course. At West Point, compass reading had been one of his best subjects, and he'd never got old Troop C lost once during the war.

He thought of the saloon in Fairhope and wondered if it had a good chop counter. He hoped the whisky would be smooth instead of the usual rotgut. Maybe they even had dancing girls. Stone loved to watch dancing girls.

He thought of sleeping in a clean bed after taking a hot bath. Maybe he could buy new clothes. He ought to buy a new hat but somehow couldn't bring himself to throw away his old cavalry hat. It'd been with him through the entire war, his constant companion, shielding him from sun and rain, and it still performed the same duties satisfactorily. Maybe it looked a little beat up, but lots of men wore hats in much worse shape.

The light was closer now, and it struck him as curious that there was only *one* light. If Fairhope was an entire town, why did it only have one light? Stone leaned forward in his saddle to take a better look. Maybe it was a very small town, but surely there'd be at least one decent hotel and saloon.

Sometimes the small towns were best. The people treated a man better. They didn't try to take every penny he had, as in the big towns. The only problem was that small towns seldom had dancing girls.

Stone could see the town more distinctly now. A few ramshackle buildings surrounded the light, and that's all there was. It didn't look like a town at all. It didn't even look like a settlement. His heart sank as his dreams of luxury evaporated. It looked more like a stagecoach stop than a town.

The closer he came, the worse it looked. The buildings were shacks, leaning in all directions. Fences were in need of repair, and a spotted dog ran out from behind a barn, yapping away. The light he'd seen was coming from one window, and a saddled horse was hitched to the rail.

Stone rode toward the light and dismounted. Throwing his reins over the rail, he walked toward the front door. He opened it and found himself in a small room. A husky man in his thirties sat on a chair, drinking whisky. In the corner a cowboy sat behind a glass of whisky, his face covered by the brim of his hat.

The man near the door looked up at Stone and smiled. "What can I do for you, friend?"

"This a hotel?"

"It's a hotel, stable, restaurant, saloon, and anythin' else you might need."

"Where can I put my horses?"

"In the barn across the way. You'll find grain in the barrel near the door. Want supper?"

"Please."

"It'll be on the table when you git back."

Stone walked out of the building and climbed onto his horse, riding it into the barn, the three other horses behind him. He put them in stalls and was removing the saddle from his horse when he heard the door close in the building across the way.

Peering into the darkness, he saw the lone cowboy walk unsteadily toward the horse at the rail. The cowboy's hat was low over his eyes, and he mounted up and rode away.

Stone brought grain and water to his horses, then rubbed them down with the old worn brush he carried around. Satisfied that he'd done everything necessary for the horses, he strolled out of the barn and headed for that hot meal, carrying the saddlebags containing the six thousand dollars over his shoulder.

He walked across the yard and entered the main building. The aroma of roast pork assailed his nostrils. He looked to the table where the proprietor sat alone, saw a jug of whisky and plates covered with food.

Stone pushed his hat back and sat at the table. Reaching for the jug, he filled a glass with whisky. He raised it to his lips and drank it down. It set him on fire. He coughed a few times and his face turned red.

The proprietor grinned, and most of his teeth were missing. He had a glass eye that stared off in its own direction. Hoisting his whisky, he drank it like water.

"What's yer name?" he asked.

"John Stone."

"I'm Mike Mingo."

They shook hands. Mingo looked at Stone's cavalry hat.

"That yers, or did you steal it?"

"It's mine."

"What outfit were you with?"

"Hampton Brigade."

Mingo moved his leg out from underneath the table, and it was a pegleg. "Lost it at Chickahominy. I was movin' forward with the Eleventh Alabama when the Yankees found our range with their cannons."

Stone stood, pulled up his shirt, and showed the long ugly scar underneath his left rib. "Gettysburg."

Mingo nodded. Stone sat down and resumed eating.

"What brings you out here?" Mingo asked.

Stone reached into his pocket and took out the picture of Marie. "I'm looking for her."

Mingo stared at the picture with his one good eye. "She's a helluva good lookin' woman. Yer wife?"

"We were engaged to be married. Ever see her?"

"Would've remembered if I had. What happened to her?"

"Don't know. What brings you out here?"

"Wanted to get away from the carpetbaggers."

"I was surprised when I arrived, because I thought Fairhope would be a big town since it's on the map."

"Fairhope *is* a big town. Did you think this was Fairhope? This is Mingo, named after me. I'm the mayor, the alderman, and the sole citizen, 'cept for the missus. It ain't on the map at all. We don't even have a post office. That's in Fairhope."

"Where's Fairhope?"

"About ten miles thataway." He pointed in the direction

Stone had been heading, and Stone realized his compass had been correct.

"I supply local ranches and farms with whatever they can't make or grow themselves, or don't feel like ridin' all the way into Fairhope for," Mingo explained, "and sometimes I get pilgrims like you on the way to Fairhope from Rendale. That's where yer comin' from, right? You get a look at that cowboy who was here when you arrived?"

"No."

"He sure seemed to recognize you. We was talkin' before you arrived, but as soon as you walked in the door, he got real quiet, and when you left he couldn't get out the door fast enough."

Stone recalled the cowboy hiding his face behind the brim of his hat. "What's his name?"

"Saunders."

Stone shrugged. "Don't know anybody by that name."

"He rides for the Rafter K."

Stone's hand froze in the air. "Did you say the Rafter K?"

"That's what I said."

"They have a ranch around here?"

"Their only ranch is around here."

"How'd you like to buy three horses, cheap?"

"Depends on what you call cheap."

"Let's go take a look at them."

"What's yer hurry?"

"I had a run-in with the boys from the Rafter K once."

"You best be on yer way. They're a bad crowd once they get likkered." Mingo raised himself and rested his hand on his wooden cane. "I'll git the money."

"You haven't seen the horses."

"I'd trust any man who rode for Wade Hampton."

Mingo hobbled toward a door, and Stone wolfed down his food. For all he knew, the cowboys from the Rafter K might be on their way at that moment. He rose, blew out the lantern, and pressed his back to the side of the window, drawing his Colts and looking outside.

It was pitch black, and he couldn't even see the stable

across the way. He wished he'd ridden straight by and cursed himself for his love of whisky, good food, and clean sheets.

Mingo returned to the room. "What happened to the light?"

"Safety precaution."

Mingo dropped some coins on the table. "Here's a hundred and twenty dollars for the three horses."

"They're not worth that much."

"Take the money and ride, you damned fool. Don't you know that the Rafter K is an outlaw outfit?"

Stone pocketed the money and slipped out the door, moving silently toward the barn. When he got inside, he stopped, listened, then saddled his horse.

"Sorry to disturb your rest," Stone told the animal, "but we've got to get the hell out of here."

He threw the saddlebags over the horse's back and climbed into the saddle. Touching the spurs to the horse's flanks, the horse moved toward the door. Stone held the reins with his left hand and drew a Colt with his right. If the men from the Rafter K were out there, he wanted to shoot first.

He reached the door of the barn and spurred the horse again. The horse jumped forward and galloped across the yard, heading south toward the open range, and the wind whistled past Stone's ears.

Stone couldn't go to Fairhope, because that's what Dillon would expect. All he could do was travel by night away from populated places and sleep during the day until he was far from the Rafter K range.

At least he'd eaten half a meal and drunk some whisky. He wanted to light a cigarette, but that might give him away to cowboys from the Rafter K. For all he knew, he might be riding directly toward them.

He'd have to be careful, stay off main trails, and follow his compass. It would've been so nice to sit in that shack and shoot the breeze with Mingo. He and Mingo had been in the war together, and Stone felt most comfortable with men who were veterans of the front lines.

Now he was alone on the prairie again, but the men from the Rafter K were hunting him. His horse moved across the grass, and Stone peered ahead into the blackness. Now he was glad the moon wasn't out.

He rode into the night and at one in the morning, heard cattle in the distance; he swerved to avoid them. An hour later he heard more cattle and again altered his direction.

He came to a stream, loosened the cinch on the horse, and let it drink. Then he lay on the ground and closed his eyes. He and the horse rested a while, then he tightened the cinch again and climbed into the saddle.

They continued in a southwesterly direction. As dawn approached he looked for a campsite, but visibility was so poor he couldn't see much. Finally he came to some bushes and trees and decided that'd be the place. He picketed his horse deep in the foliage, removed the saddle, and anchored it against a tree. Then he lay down and closed his eyes. A faint pink tinge was on the horizon as the dawn began to break.

He awakened in the late afternoon because the sun shone directly onto his face. Sitting up, he saw the skeleton of a man twenty feet in front of him in the middle of the clearing. He stared at the skeleton for a few moments, then rose and walked toward it.

The skeleton lay on its back, its hollow eyes staring blankly at the sky. An old brown arrow, bent by time, lay among the ribs. It wore no clothes or anything else. The Indians had taken everything.

Stone kneeled beside the skeleton and lit a cigarette. He wondered who he was and what mad dream he'd been following when the Indians shot the arrow into his heart. He'd probably been scalped and mutilated, too. Stone wanted to get moving but knew he should stay hidden until dark.

He moved his saddle and belongings to a spot where he couldn't see the skeleton and finished his cigarette. Then he visited his horse and moved him to where there was more grass.

Stone sat on the ground and looked at his map. Fairhope was behind him now, but there was another town named Beverly about forty miles away in the direction of where he hoped to intersect the wagon train.

He doubted that the men from the Rafter K would go that far to catch him. Maybe he could get the clean bed, bath, and good meal that he craved.

Stone saddled his horse when it was dark and set out again, this time heading for Beverly. He rode all night, slept the next day in a cave cut into a butte, and had traveled half the night when he came to the top of a hill and saw below him a scattering of lights twinkling and sparkling in the midst of an enormous open range.

His mouth watered as he thought of a steak dinner and good whisky. He could stay in the best hotel in town with all the money he had. He hoped the cowboys from the Rafter K weren't in town but didn't feel like hiding anymore. He'd slept on the ground enough.

The town came closer, and he could see it was no Mingo. Buildings two and three stories high were spread over several blocks, and the downtown area glowed brightly. The buildings were painted and in good repair. Stone rode onto the main street of Beverly, looking for the hotel.

He passed private homes and businesses closed for the night, then came to the downtown area. There were three noisy saloons and one boxy hotel with a sign in front that said:

BEVERLY HOTEL

The stable was next door, and he rode inside, dismounting, throwing the two sets of saddlebags over his shoulder. A young man in a floppy hat came out of the shadows, carrying a lantern.

"I'll take 'im," he said, grasping the horse's reins. "Where you comin' in from?"

"Mingo."

"How's old Mike?"

"Seemed like his leg was bothering him."

"That's what I thought last time I saw him. God damn Yankees. I see you were in the war, too."

"Hampton Brigade."

"Fifth Mississippi."

They saluted each other, not with regulation salutes but rather the casual greeting of two old soldiers in a barn at night on the frontier.

"Cowboys from the Rafter K come to Beverly often?"

"Not too often."

"I'll be staying across the street at the hotel. If you see any riders from the Rafter K, I'd appreciate it if you'd let me know. I had a run-in with them a while back, and they might try to kill me." Stone took out a coin and tossed it to the man.

The man tossed it back. "Keep yer money, pardner. Pay when you leave. What's yer name?"

"John Stone."

"Chip Flanagan."

"You got dancing girls in this town?"

"The Gold Dust Saloon."

Stone walked across the street to the Beverly Hotel, a big, wooden, planked box with windows. It had no veranda, and Stone passed directly from the boardwalk through the door and into the lobby, where a man with a long, curved, black mustache and his hair parted in the middle leaned on the counter and read a newspaper. In the far corner, a man in a suit lay sprawled on a chair and snored like a foghorn.

"Room for the night," Stone said to the man behind the counter. "Can I get a bath?"

The man winked. "You can get anything at all you want."

"I'd like to take a bath."

"I'll have one prepared for you. Anything else?" He leaned forward and said softly, "Women?"

"No thank you."

Stone took the key and climbed the stairs to his room on the second floor. He opened the door and entered a small room with a bed, washstand, thick heavy dresser, closet, and chair. He dropped the saddlebags onto the floor and walked to the window, looking to the street. He could see men coming and going from the saloons, some accompanied by women. A drunken cowboy on a horse rode by, and the cowboy was so loose in the saddle he was barely hanging on.

Stone sat on the chair and rolled a cigarette. The walls were plain unpainted wood and carried no pictures, and the bed was large enough for two. Stone stared longingly at the bed. He hadn't slept in a bed for nearly a month.

There was a knock on the door. He yanked a Colt, pulled the doorknob, and saw an old black woman in a bandanna. "Yer bath is ready, sir."

Stone handed her a coin, placed his hat on the bedpost, and carried his saddlebags down the hall to the bathroom. He undressed, climbed into the tub, and closed his eyes.

Deep fatigue came over him as the hot water soaked into his skin and warmed the marrow of his bones. His joints relaxed, and he breathed in the steam rising from the water. He could feel the dirt and filth, sweat and dust, fall away from his body.

It reminded him of before the war, when he took a hot bath every day, and sometimes twice a day. He hadn't realized at the time that he'd been living like a prince in a castle, but now that he was a vagabond on the frontier, he understood.

Servants had done whatever he asked. It amused him to order grown adults around when he'd been a small boy, but his mother smacked him when she found out about it and told him to stop. All he did was play. When he became older, his life revolved around hunting, drinking, and parties. It had been idyllic, and the most beautiful girl in the county had been in love with him.

He thought of Marie wearing one of her ball gowns, a ribbon in her hair, dancing across the floor, her arms held out gracefully. No one had ever made him feel as alive as she. That's why he needed her. He felt like half a man without her.

He finished the bath, put on clean clothes, and carried

the saddlebags down the hall to his room. He sat on the chair and smoked another cigarette. He'd intended to go to a saloon, but fatigue had caught up with him. His eyes were heavy-lidded and there was a dull ache in his shoulders. It was around two in the morning, and he thought he should go to bed.

There was a knock on the door. He rose, pulled out a Colt, and opened the door quickly.

A young woman not more than twenty stood there in a low-cut purple gown. Her hair was straight and jet black, and she was five feet five. She reached into her purse and came out with a bottle of whisky. "Care for a drink?"

Stone looked at the bottle and thought a drink would help him sleep. "Don't mind if I do."

She entered his room and sat on the bed, crossing her legs, producing two glasses from her purse. She handed him one, then filled both glasses with dark amber whisky.

"Down the hatch," she said.

They both drank whisky, and it was the usual rotgut made in somebody's barn. Stone looked at her, and her legs were showing up to her knees. Her eyes were almond-shaped and her mouth a rosebud.

"Where you from?" she asked.

"South Carolina."

"I'm from Maine. Gets real cold in Maine. Want to go to bed?"

"No thank you."

She was surprised. "Don't think I'm pretty?"

"I'm engaged to get married."

"I been married twice and got three kids, but what's that got to do with it?"

"How old are you?"

"Seventeen."

She stood and reached to her side, unfastening a button. Then she unfastened another button, tossing her head wantonly. She unfastened the next, and Stone stared in astonishment as her dress peeled away.

She wore nothing underneath, and her body was a perfect flowing of curves and hollows with milky white skin, and her breasts round and ripe-looking. He hadn't seen a naked woman since he last saw Marie, and the animal inside him felt lust. He rose from the chair and looked at her, wanting to take her in his arms.

She smiled and walked toward him, reaching out, and he took a step back. Laughing, she rushed toward him and wrapped her arms around him, holding him tightly against her.

She wore an exotic French perfume, and it made him dizzy. She raised her face to him and pursed her lips.

"Let's do it, honey."

Stone felt himself going weak in the knees. She was right there, ready, and who knew where Marie was? And he needed it. He'd been alone for so long. He could have that wonderful thrill again.

"Make up your mind," she said. "I don't have all night."

In a flash Stone's mood changed. She was a prostitute, this was her job, she didn't care about him at all beyond what he had in his pocket.

He raised his hands to her shoulders and gently pushed her away. "Please put on your clothes," he said.

He sat on the chair and rolled a cigarette. She put on her dress sadly. "I do somethin' wrong?" she asked like a guilty child.

Stone looked at her and realized that's what she was: a guilty child.

"What do you charge?" Stone asked.

"Four dollars."

Stone reached into his jeans, took out the coins, and handed them to her.

"What's this for?"

"Buy your kids something on me."

She looked at him for a few moments, then stepped forward and kissed his cheek. "Thanks."

She walked out of the room, and Stone smoked his cigarette, still inhaling her fragrance. If she hadn't put him off, he would've gone through with it. That's how close it had been.

He realized his willpower wasn't what he'd thought.

Maybe one day he'd give in, and then it would never be the same with him and Marie. He looked at the bed in front of him, fluffy and white, and a deep exhaustion came over him, the result of insufficient sleep. This was the moment he'd been dreaming about while sitting atop his horse in the middle of nowhere. At last he'd sleep on a real bed.

He took off his clothes, pulled a Colt out of a holster, blew out the lamp, and crawled into bed, the Colt in his right hand and his finger curled around the trigger.

He let himself sink into the mattress, and it was like dropping through a cloud. No pebbles ground into his hip. His head was on a soft pillow instead of a hard saddle, and the sheets smelled sweet and clean, unlike the horsey smell of his saddle.

His body went limp and in seconds he was asleep.

There was a loud, insistent knock, and Stone woke suddenly out of a deep slumber, bringing his gun around and pointing it at the door.

"John Stone—open up!"

Stone got out of bed and opened the door. Standing before him was Chip Flanagan from the stable, greatly agitated. Flanagan entered the room and said, "Horses from the Rafter K're in town. I was on my way home from work, and I saw 'em. They're lookin' for you. You better clear out of here. I got yer horse in back."

Stone got dressed quickly, strapped on his guns, and pulled on his boots. He put on his hat, threw the saddlebags over his shoulder, and walked to the door, opening it cautiously, peering into the corridor.

It was darkness interlaced with rays of moonlight shining through the windows at the ends of the corridor. The stairwell glowed with light from the lobby downstairs. Stone turned to Flanagan behind him.

"I'll go first. You wait a few minutes, then go home. Thanks for your help."

Stone stepped into the corridor and walked softly to the stairs, descending them to the lobby, holding his pistols ready to fire. In the lobby a few well-dressed drunks lolled on upholstered chairs, and the clerk was behind his desk, writing something. Stone crossed the lobby, looking for ways to get to the back of the building without going outside. He saw several doors, and the clerk looked up, his eyes widening at the sight of the two guns in Stone's hands.

"May I help you, sir?"

"Is there a back entrance?"

"Over there."

Stone opened a door and passed down a long dark corridor lined with doors. Another door was at the end, and it had a small window. He looked outside and saw his horse tied to the rail, saddled and ready to go. Stone smiled and thought gratefully of Chip Flanagan. He opened the door and stepped outside.

"That's him!"

The world around him exploded with gunfire, bullets crashing into the wooden structure of the building, splinters flying in the air. Stone slammed the door shut and ran down the corridor toward the lobby.

He charged into the lobby just as a group of cowboys were entering the front door, guns in their hands.

"Get him!"

Stone fired four fast shots then ran for the stairs, leaping up several at a time as bullets whizzed around him and one hit the saddlebags full of coins on his shoulder, causing him to lose his balance. He spun around, fell to the stairs, and fired four shots at the cowboys rushing to the stairs below him.

They dived for cover, and Stone vaulted up the stairs to the next landing. He paused, fired a few shots at the cowboys, then ran around and climbed the next flight of stairs to the third floor of the hotel.

Behind him he could hear the boots of the cowboys scrambling to climb the stairs and kill him. Again he cursed his affection for clean sheets, hot baths, and dancing girls. *I should've slept on the prairie, but like a damn fool, I had to come here.*

He came to the third floor, and it was a dark corridor

with a window at each end. He tried all the doors on the corridor, and they were locked until he came to one near the end. The door opened. He stepped silently inside the room and smelled thick, alcoholic fumes. A stout man in his fifties wearing long underwear lay passed out drunk on the bed, snoring loudly. Stone locked the door and pressed his ear against it.

He heard the cowboys from the Rafter K in the hallway.

"Where the hell is he!" roared the voice of Dillon, ramrod of the brand.

"He's up here someplace!" somebody replied.

"Find him!"

Stone crossed the room to the window and looked down at a dark alley and the next building, which was only two stories high, with a peaked roof. He could jump out the window to the roof next door, but the roof looked awfully steep, and he might slide off.

If only I had a rope. But his rope was affixed to his saddle. The drunk on the bed continued to snore, and Stone stepped back to the door, pressing his ear against it and listening.

"He must've gone into one of these rooms!" somebody said.

"Knock on all the doors!" Dillon replied. "If nobody answers, shoot out the locks! Don't let the son of a bitch get away!"

Stone stepped back from the door and looked at the roof across the way. It was a long jump, and he didn't think he could make it. He realized he was trapped and broke out into a cold sweat.

From the corridor he could hear cowboys pounding on doors with the butts of their guns, hollering, "Open up!" He heard shots and realized they were blowing away the locks on some of the doors. Stone thought of only one thing to do.

He crawled underneath the bed and hastily reloaded both his Colts, then lay still and waited. The man snored in the bed above him, and Stone heard shots and a commotion in the corridor.

"What's the meaning of this!" shouted an indignant female voice.

"Shut up and stand against that wall!"

Stone knew they'd get to his room pretty soon. He'd gone through five years of war, and it looked as though he was going to get shot down in a hotel room on the frontier. He racked his brain and tried to think of something else to do, but there was nothing except try to get as many of them as possible.

There was a knock on the door followed by, "Open up!"

The drunk missed a beat in his snoring then resumed. The cowboy knocked again. Then a shot was fired and the door was kicked open. Light entered the room from the corridor, where one of the cowboys was carrying a lantern. The man on top of the bed continued to snore.

"Look at this guy!" said the cowboy. "He's so drunk he can't hear nothin'."

"Look in the closet and underneath the bed," said Dillon.

Stone tensed and tightened his fingers around the triggers. He heard two sets of footsteps approaching. One set went to the closet, and the other approached the bed. Stone looked at two boots in the light beside the bed. The ankles in the boots flexed and then a pair of knees appeared. Stone took aim with the gun in his right hand, and a second later a face looked at him sideways.

Stone pulled the trigger of the gun, and the face cracked apart. Stone rolled out from underneath the bed and fired both his guns at the cowboys in the doorway as he jumped to his feet. He leapt over the bed as the drunken man still slept soundly on top of the bedspread, and then the cowboys got over their surprise.

"Kill him!" hollered Dillon.

There was only one place to go. Stone clenched his teeth, lowered his head, and dived toward the window as bullets slammed into the wall around him. He crashed through the glass and sailed through the air in a long parabola, landing with shards of glass on the roof of the house across the alley.

He dug into the wooden shingles with his fingernails and the tips of his boots, slid down a few inches, and came to a stop. Turning around, he saw faces in the broken window above him. He raised his Colts and fired, and the faces disappeared.

Taking a deep breath, he climbed up the side of the roof as a bullet struck the shingle a few inches from his left ear, and another bullet landed beside his left hip. Scrambling frantically, he made it to the top of the roof and lunged over.

Bullets whacked into the roof, but now he was sheltered. Pausing, loading his Colts, he heard more bullets being fired, and then Dillon's voice: "Git the son of a bitch!"

Stone thought the shooting should've attracted the law by now. Climbing down the side of the roof, he came to the eave and looked to the ground. It was two stories down, nearly twenty feet, a long drop into a dark alley, but he had no place else to go.

As a boy, he'd climbed trees and jumped off branches, but never at a distance like this. A man could break bones from this height, but a bullet would be far more lethal. All he could do was roll when he hit the ground to cushion the shock.

He threw the saddlebags over the eave, then took a deep breath and jumped, his spurs gleaming in the light of the moon. He sailed through the air, his stomach rising into his throat, and floated toward the ground, passing windows and clapboard shingles on the wall across the way. He knew he had to be loose when he hit the ground, otherwise his thigh bones would burst through his hips, and he would be helpless before the men from the Rafter K.

He looked down and saw the murky depths of the alley coming up fast. The saddlebags struck the ground, and Stone crashed down a second later with such force that the wind was knocked out of him. He opened his eyes and found himself lying on his back, both guns still in his hands.

His ankles and kneebones hurt, and so did his rear end, but he didn't think anything was broken. Getting to his feet, he threw the saddlebags over his shoulder and ran down the alley toward the street.

It was deserted, and the music had stopped in the saloons. The townspeople were in hiding.

"Where's the sheriff!" Stone shouted.

"Out of town!" somebody replied behind an open window.

A crowd of cowboys spilled out of the Beverly Hotel, and Dillon, wearing his his black leather frock coat, was in front of them. "There he is!" Dillon hollered. "Get him!"

The cowboys took aim and fired, and Stone ducked back into the alley. He ran toward the backyard and turned left, hoping to make a run for his horse behind the Beverly Hotel. Bolting across the backyard of the next building, he came to the rear of the hotel, and the horse was there, guarded by two men.

"Who's there!" one of them demanded, peering into the night.

Stone rushed toward him and opened fire. The cowboy saw Stone at the last moment, before he could take aim, and Stone's bullets ripped into him. The other cowboy got off a wild shot before Stone drilled him in the lower abdomen, and the cowboy fell to the ground screaming, clutching his groin.

Stone heard pounding footsteps behind him and spun around. A crowd of cowboys charged toward him through the alley. Stone dropped to one knee and fired both his guns, one after the other, aiming and firing into the cowboys caught in the narrow alleyway. They hollered and fell to the ground, some hit by bullets, some hiding from the rain of lead.

Both of Stone's guns went empty at the same time, and if he tried to climb onto his horse, they'd shoot him out of the saddle. He packed the guns into their holsters and jumped a four-foot fence, landing in the backyard of the next building. Cowboys from the Rafter K rushed toward the yard and opened fire. Bullets whistled all around Stone, and there was only one place to go. He ran toward the back of the building and hurled himself at the window, covering his face with his arms, and burst through the glass, becoming entangled in a thick brocade curtain, falling to the floor in a heap.

He tore the curtain away and found himself in a small library with shelves of books on all the walls and a desk with a chair in front of it. He pulled open the door and charged down a dark corridor that led to the front of the building.

He came to the huge front room, and over the fireplace was a rifle. He plucked it down and looked at it in the moonlight streaming through the window. It was a Henry, and he hoped it was loaded. He jacked the lever twice, and a cartridge flew out of the chamber. Loading it back into the slot, he lay the rifle on a chair then thumbed cartridges into his Colts.

It was a helluva time for the sheriff to be out of town. Stone looked out the window and realized his only hope was to steal a horse and ride it as hard as he could.

"Drop your guns!"

Stone looked up and saw a bald-headed, short man in a robe pointing a double-barrelled shotgun at him.

"A group of drunken cowboys are after me," Stone said, "and the sheriff is out of town."

Just then they heard movement and voices coming from the backyard through the broken window.

"He went in here!" somebody shouted.

The man took a step forward and looked at Stone's face. "Hide in that closet," he said. "I won't give you away."

Stone moved in long swift strides toward the closet and stepped inside, while the man opened the front door a crack. The closet contained coats, and some gave off the fragrance of women's perfume. Stone moved into the folds of fabric, holding the rifle aimed at the door. The first cowboy who opened it would die, and then it would be down and dirty to the bitter end.

The cowboys entered the building through the broken rear window, and Stone could hear them moving cautiously down the corridor. This was the first time he'd stopped since Flanagan woke him up, and he was gasping for breath, his face covered with perspiration and his shirt sticking to his skin.

The cowboys crowded into the main living room on the other side of the door.

"Where is he?" one of them asked.

"Went out the front door." the man replied. "Headed across the street."

"Now wait a minute," another voice said. "I was standin' outside, and I didn't see anybody come out."

Then came Dillon's voice: "Search the building."

"Now just a minute," the man said. "You can't just walk in here and do whatever you want."

"Shut up!" said Dillon.

Stone held the barrel of the Henry pointed at the door, his finger tight around the trigger and rivulets of perspiration on his face. He heard footsteps moving throughout the main floor of the building, climbing the stairs. One set of footsteps approached the door of the closet, and Stone got ready. The doorknob twisted, the door opened, and Stone fired at the cowboy standing in front of him.

The bullet struck the cowboy in the chest, and Stone charged out of the closet, jumped over the falling cowboy, took two huge bounding leaps as bullets were fired wildly at him, and crashed through the living room window, landing on the boardwalk outside.

A hitching post was directly in front of him, but unfortunately no horses were tied there. No horses were across the street, either, but many horses were tied to hitching rails near the hotels and saloons in the center of town. "I've got to get a horse," he muttered and then heard gunshots behind him. A bullet stuck the saddlebags full of coins over his shoulders, knocking him off balance. He fell to the ground, rolled over, and lay on his stomach in the middle of the street, raising the rifle to his shoulder. He lined up the sights on one of the cowboys running for cover, squeezed the trigger, and the rifle bucked against his shoulder. A cloud of smoke rose in the air, and the cowboy fell onto his face.

Bullets kicked into the ground all around Stone as he lay in the street firing back. The cowboys shot guns at him, but the rifle was the more accurate weapon at that distance. Stone aimed at the opening in an alley, and when a cowboy hat showed, he aimed at the eye underneath and pulled the trigger. The cowboy screamed and fell sideways out of the alley.

"Get him from the other side!" Dillon shouted.

Stone was in the wide open and knew he was in danger of being caught in a crossfire. He looked longingly at the horses in front of the saloons, but they were a long way off. The alleyway behind him was closer. Maybe he could get into it and find a horse back there.

He jumped to his feet and ran to the alley quickly, and the cowboys fired at him, but it was dark and he moved perpendicular to them, presenting a difficult target. He heard their bullets and felt dirt kicked into his face, but then he was in the alley running toward the rear of the buildings.

He came to the end of the alley, and no cowboys were there, but neither were any horses. He decided to continue heading away from the center of town. Running to the next row of houses, he noticed a red light in the window of a two-story building.

He ran toward the door beside the window, glancing over his shoulder, but no cowboys came after him; they were wary now that he had a rifle. Rushing toward the door, he opened it and stepped inside a small, dark, smoke-filled room filled with cowboys and whores kissing and squirming against each other. He knew at a glance it wasn't the best whorehouse in town.

A heavyset prostitute wearing a red low-cut dress walked toward him, holding a glass of whisky. "What can I do for you, cowboy?"

"Want a woman."

"Take yer pick."

"How about you?"

"Me?" She laughed. "I'm the boss. I don't sleep with the customers. Who else you want?"

"Anybody."

"You sound hot to trot. How about Elyssa here?"

She put her arm around a woman in her mid-twenties with wavy black hair who looked as if she might have some Mexican or Italian blood.

"Let's go upstairs," Stone said to her, taking her by the arm.

They walked together toward the stairs, and he didn't take his eyes off the door. She looked at his profile and noticed his concern.

"Somebody after you?" she asked.

"Yes."

"Hurry up. My room's just around the corner."

She hiked up her skirts and ran quickly up the stairs, and Stone followed, passing a drunken cowboy staggering downstairs, buttoning his fly. They came to the second floor, walked swiftly down a corridor lined with doors, and she unlocked one of them.

He followed her into a room that had a bed and a gigantic mirror facing it. She locked the door and turned around to face him.

"What have you done?"

"Some cowboys from the Rafter K are after me. They want to kill me."

"They're a bad bunch," she said. "Sit down. You look as if you need a drink."

She opened the bottom drawer of the dresser and took out a bottle as he walked toward the back window, stood to the side, and looked outside.

The only light spilled out the windows of the building, and he couldn't see anything in the backyard. Evidently he'd lost them for the time being.

She poured two glasses of whisky. "I had a boyfriend once who'd been an outlaw," she said. "I know what it's like to be on the dodge. What's yer name?"

"John Stone."

"Why's the Rafter K mad at you?"

"I killed a few of 'em. Do you know where I can get a horse?"

"I can get you my horse."

"That'd be too dangerous. It's even dangerous for you here. Maybe you should go downstairs. I'll give you some money."

He reached into his pocket, and she placed her hand on his wrist. "Stop that," she said. "You don't have to pay me. Relax. Have a drink."

He sat on the chair again, and she dropped onto the bed. He picked up the glass of whisky and took a gulp.

"Where are you from?" she asked.

"My last stop was Mingo."

"You sound like yer from the south. So am I. I grew up in Tennessee. We had a farm, but then we came out here, and my father got killed by the goddamned Indians."

The sound of chaos and confusion came to them from downstairs. Elyssa walked to the door and opened it a crack.

"What the hell do you think yer doin'?" said the madam, her gravelly voice channeled up the stairs and through the hallway.

"I'm lookin' for a man about this tall!" said Dillon, and Stone imagined him holding his hand at Stone's approximate height. "He come in here?"

"About half the men in here look like that."

"Search the rooms!" Dillon said to his men.

Elyssa closed the door and locked it. "Get into bed!"

Stone moved toward the window, pressed his back against the wall, and moved the drapes slightly so he could look into the yard. He saw three cowboys with their guns trained on the back door.

"I said get in bed," she told him, stepping out of her dress.

She hung it over a chair and wrapped a silk robe around her shoulders. Stone heard footsteps on the stairs, spreading out on the corridor outside the door. They heard a knock.

"Who's there?" she asked.

"Open the door or I'll shoot the lock!" a man replied.

She pulled down the covers of the bed, and Stone got

between the sheets, aiming his guns at the door. Elyssa opened it.

"Don't you know yer disturbin' the peace?" she asked jovially.

"Out of my way!"

Stone heard her being pushed to the side, and footsteps moved toward the center of the room.

"Come out from underneath them sheets!" the voice said.

Stone aimed both Colts in the direction of the voice and pulled the triggers. His guns exploded simultaneously, and the bullets blew the sheet off him. It fell away and Stone saw a cowboy staggering in the middle of the room and other cowboys near the door.

Stone leapt out of the bed and fired at the cowboys at the door as bullets thudded into the mattress. Two cowboys at the door fell back, their bodies peppered with holes, and Elyssa ran into the closet as whores screamed downstairs. Stone pulled over the dresser and crouched behind it, thumbing cartridges into his guns.

He couldn't jump out the back window because they had the whorehouse surrounded. He couldn't go out the front door because that's where Dillon and his men were. The dresser he crouched behind was flimsy. A head appeared in the doorway and Stone fired, but the head pulled back in time.

"He's in there behind some furniture," somebody said.

"Rush him!"

"You rush him, Dillon. I ain't stickin' my neck out anymore."

"Somebody get a torch. We'll smoke the son of a bitch out."

Stone heard somebody running down the stairs. He looked at the window, looked at the door, and wished there were another way. If they set the room on fire, he was finished.

The bottle of whisky was nearby. He reached for it and took a swig to steady his hands. He'd always told himself that if he ever was faced with death, he wanted to die fighting, and now his time had come.

He saw his whole life flash before his eyes. *I'm too young to die*, he thought, but he'd known men younger than he who'd died. He thought back to Crawford and the fight he'd gotten into with the men from the Rafter K. He knew if he had to do it over again, he'd do it the same way.

He aimed his guns at the door. Footsteps approached down the corridor, and a flaming torch was thrown into the room. Stone looked at it, and it was the leg of a chair with one end burning, giving off the smell of coal oil. It lay on the rug, and soon the rug was afire also, curls of black smoke rising toward the ceiling.

The door of the closet opened, and Elyssa screamed, "Fire!"

"Dillon!" Stone shouted. "Let the woman out!"

"Send 'er through!" Dillon replied. "We ain't after her!"

Elyssa came out of the closet, took one look at Stone, then ran out the door. A second later a cowboy's head appeared, and he fired a wild shot at Stone, who fired back, but Stone's shot wasn't wild. The cowboy hollered, a bullet in his bicep, and he spun out of the doorway.

"Relax!" Dillon said to his men. "We ain't in no rush! He's gotta come out sooner or later!"

Stone looked as the flame spread over the rug, part of which was beneath the bed. The fire licked at the sheet and blanket, and now they were on fire, too. The room filled with smoke, and Stone coughed. An ashtray lay on the floor, and he threw it at the window, breaking the glass, and a moment later bullets from the guns of the cowboys outside flew into the room.

Stone pulled his bandanna over his nose. He could see the end coming. The smoke would force him to rush the door, and they'd cut him down. Or he'd jump out the window, and they'd fill him full of holes before he hit the ground.

He coughed again and tried to make up his mind about which to choose but then realized it didn't matter. He was going to die no matter what he did.

He decided he'd rather take as many of them with him as he could, so it'd be the door. He'd jump up and rush it in a few more moments when the smoke got too thick.

The smoke rose and formed a large cloud underneath the ceiling. The cloud expanded and got lower every second, and when it reached Stone, it'd suffocate him. He prepared to make his last charge.

A voice hollered: "Dillon, there's a posse comin'!"

There was a pause, then Stone could hear Dillon: "How many men?"

"Fifty, at least."

"Let's get out of here!" Dillon bellowed. "Bring the horses around!"

Stone heard them running down the stairs. He looked out the window and saw a crowd of armed citizens approaching the rear of the whorehouse. The cowboys who'd been outside had run away. Then he heard gunfire at the front of the whorehouse, and someone screamed orders. It sounded like the war.

A solid wall of flame flickered in front of him, its heat searing his face. He covered his face with his arms, stood on the dresser, and jumped through the fire, feeling intense heat all over his body for a split second. The fire warmed his back as he peered into the empty corridor. A fusillade of gunfire erupted outside.

He stepped into the corridor, both his guns cocked and leveled and made his way to the stairs. Doors lining the corridor were open, revealing disheveled beds and clothes strewn everywhere. He could smell gunsmoke mixed with ladies' perfume. As he descended the stairs, he saw the Beverly Volunteer Fire Brigade run into the downstairs parlor carrying buckets of water, looking around excitedly.

"The fire's up here!" Stone called out to them.

They ran up the stairs in a long file, water dripping from the buckets onto the bare wooden planks, and Stone passed them on the way down. He came to the parlor and saw a bottle of whisky and some glasses on a table. He walked toward it, poured a glass, drank some, then dropped onto a chair and rolled a cigarette.

He let himself go. Adrenaline still pumped through his arteries, and his heart beat rapidly. He lit the cigarette and inhaled deeply. Footsteps came to him from outside, and then a man with a badge appeared in the doorway.

"Are you the one they were after?" he asked Stone.

"Yes."

"What's yer name?"

"John Stone."

The man with the badge was followed into the parlor by several armed townspeople, including the man whose library Stone had broken into.

"I'm Deputy Atterberry. What you do to them boys to make 'em so mad?"

"One of them said something I didn't like."

"They're a bad bunch, the Rafter K. We got most of 'em, but a few got away. Have to ask you to come to the sheriff's office to fill out an affidavit. How come yer in Beverly?"

"I'm looking for a wagon train," Stone said.

After leaving the sheriff's office, Stone walked into the Gold Dust Saloon. Straight ahead against the far wall was a darkened stage, and before it were tables and chairs, about a third filled with men and a few women, the latter most probably prostitutes.

Stone strolled toward the bar, his saddlebags over his shoulder and his rifle in his left hand. The bartender wore a goatee and his head was shaved. "What can I do for you?"

"Any more dancing girls tonight?"

"Last show was at midnight."

"Whisky."

The bartender poured a glass, and Stone carried it to a table against the wall. He lay his rifle on the table and sat down heavily, pushing back his hat. Then he raised the glass to his lips.

He opened one of his saddlebags, took out his map, and tried to figure out where the wagon train was. He made some calculations, then some measurements, and marked a cross on the map. The wagon train would be somewhere in the middle of Indian Territory, and Stone figured he'd catch up with it in two or three days if he left first thing in the morning.

He put the map away and leaned back in the chair, wondering if he should spend the night in the hotel, between clean sheets, or sleep on the prairie where it'd be harder for somebody to find him.

Then he flashed on his horse. The last time he'd seen him, he was tied up in back of the Beverly Hotel, saddled and ready to go. Probably he was still there unless somebody brought him to the stable. Stone thought he'd better find the horse before he was stolen.

Stone gulped down the rest of the whisky and walked out of the saloon. He'd missed the dancing girls and felt disappointed. There was nothing like dancing girls to lighten a man's heart.

He stepped outside and crossed the street, heading for the alley beside the Beverly Hotel. This was the scene of his fight against the Rafter K hands, but now it was dark and peaceful, and the only people out were drunks sleeping on benches.

He passed through the alley, hearing his footsteps echoing off the walls. The end of the alley opened onto a backyard, and Stone saw his horse at the rail, the saddle on his back. Stone smiled, because that particular horse always had a lot of patience.

Stone heard a faint metallic *snick* sound behind him and dropped to the ground. A split second later a gun fired, and a bullet whisked over his head. Stone saw a man in a doorway, aimed his rifle, and pumped four shots into him. The man hunched over, dropped his gun, leaned to the side, and fell to the ground.

Stone ran toward him, the rifle in his hands ready to fire, and saw Dillon lying on the ground, wearing his black leather frock coat, but with blood all over it. Dillon's eyes were closed and blood trickled out of his mouth. Stone's volleys had stuck him in the chest, and he'd been dead before he hit the ground.

Stone glanced around cautiously. He recalled Deputy Atterberry telling him some men from the Rafter K had got away. Kneeling beside Dillon's body, peering into the darkness, he didn't see anything suspicious. He reasoned that if more men from the Rafter K were around, they would've fired with Dillon when Stone had been in the open.

Dillon had probably been alone, too filled with hatred to run away with the rest of them. He'd stayed behind to bushwhack Stone, but it hadn't turned out that way.

Stone walked back toward his horse, untied him, then climbed into the saddle, pushing the rifle into its boot. He pulled the reins and wheeled the horse, then put the spurs to him and headed south toward Indian Territory.

12

IT WAS MORNING, and the wagon train was a few miles north of the Texas border. The women prepared breakfast, while the men checked the wagons and horses for the long day of travel that lay ahead.

"Somebody's comin'!" shouted Stewart Donahue.

Taggart looked in the direction Donahue was pointing and saw in the distant flats the shimmering figure of a man on a horse. Taggart ran to the rear of his wagon and pulled his spyglass out of a bag. Raising it to his eye, he focused on the figure in the distance. Gradually the image became sharper. A big man sat on the horse, and Taggart would know those wide shoulders anywhere.

"It's him!"

The travelers gathered on the side of the campsite that faced the oncoming rider. Jason Fenwick broke away from the others and ran across the grass toward Stone.

"Did you git my money!"

A deep bellowing cavalry officer's voice came back to him over the hills and flats. "I got it!"

Fenwick jumped for joy then ran back to his wife, wrapped his arms around her, and kissed her cheek. Together they danced a jig like a couple of lunatics.

Stone rode closer, sitting squarely on his saddle, a cigarette dangling out the corner of his mouth and his hat low over his eyes. He'd been on the trail for three days longer than he'd thought, but he'd finally found the wagon train.

The travelers surrounded Stone, who pulled the saddle-bags full of money off the rear of his horse and threw it at Fenwick.

The saddlebags fell to the ground, and Fenwick opened the flap eagerly. Thrusting his hand inside, he came out with a handful of money. He'd been the richest man on the wagon train, then the poorest, and now he was the richest again.

Stone climbed down from his horse, and Taggart walked up to him. "Where'd you find 'em?"

Stone pointed in a northeasterly direction. "Somewhere out there on the way to Rendale."

"What happened?"

"I'll tell you after I get some shut-eye."

Stone watered his horse and tied him to the rear of Taggart's wagon. Then he climbed into the back of the wagon and lay down. In seconds he was asleep.

He slept all day, as the wagon train rumbled across the plains. Taggart rode up front as scout, and Cornelius Donahue drove Taggart's wagon. Stone awoke in mid-afternoon and raised his head above the tailgate of the wagon. He saw the next wagon, driven by the Reverend Joshua McGhee, with his wife Doris and daughter Alice seated on either side of him.

His eyes met the eyes of Alice McGhee through the billowing dust. Lying down again, he rolled a cigarette. He wanted a cup of coffee but would have to wait until the wagon train stopped.

He felt restless after a few miles. Climbing forward, he sat on the front seat next to Cornelius Donahue, a young man with blond hair and a wholesome, innocent face.

"I'll take those reins for a while," Stone said.

Cornelius handed him the reins, and Stone felt the brute power of the horses pulling the wagon. Up ahead, Taggart was a tiny dot on the plains. Stone was surprised that the wagon train had experienced no serious difficulties with Indians yet.

The sun became hotter as the wagon train traveled south. Stone's body became coated with a thin layer of perspiration. He sipped from the canteen lying in the boot.

Taggart rode back to the wagon train in the late afternoon. He saw Stone on the front seat and grinned wearily. "Glad to see you up. Looks like we got a problem. The water hole ahead is dry."

"Where's the next one?" Stone asked.

"About twelve miles. We won't reach it today. You feel well enough to ride?"

"Yes."

"Take my horse."

Taggart clambered down from his horse to the wagon and sat on the other side of Cornelius Donahue. Then Stone jumped onto Taggart's horse. He touched his spurs to the animal's flanks, and it trotted forward.

The wind pressed against Stone's shirt and cooled him down; he still was stiff and sore from his long ride back to the wagon train. He examined the terrain for signs of Indians, but all he could see were limitless vistas. Then he came to the dry water hole Taggart had spoken of.

Trees and bushes surrounding the water hole were dying from lack of water. Stone dismounted and touched his hand to the sand at the bottom of the water hole, and it was bone dry. He dug down a few inches, and it was dry there, too. Stone took off his hat and wiped his forehead with the back of his hand. This was their first dry water hole. He hoped the next one wouldn't be dry, too.

Stone looked at his map. The next water was a river. He put his map away and climbed onto his horse, urging it forward. Thinking about water made him thirsty, but he decided not to drink. The time had come to start rationing water.

The sun sank low in the west, and long shadows appeared on the plains. Stone's horse ambled over the grass, and Stone knew the horse was thirsty, too. No clouds were in the sky, which meant no hope of rain. Stone's mouth felt dry as sand.

The light became dimmer and then it became dark. Stone could hear the wagon train behind him, rattling and clanking across the terrain. Usually they would make camp at dusk, but today they pressed on in their search for water. A wild dog barked not far away. Stone thought about Wayne Collins tied up at his campsite. *Coyotes probably got him by now.*

Stone rode on into the night. The air became cooler and the stars shone brightly overhead.

A stand of trees loomed up out of the darkness, and Stone realized it was the river. But he couldn't hear the rush of water, and that was a bad sign. Stone passed through the trees that lined the river and continued down the slope. It was dark at the bottom, and he couldn't see whether it was water or dirt. His horse wasn't hurrying, and that was another bad sign. The horse would've smelled the water and quickened his pace if it was there.

Stone came to the edge of the river; there was no water. He dismounted and walked onto the river bottom. The dirt and stones were dry. He lifted a sizable stone and placed his hand underneath it to determine whether there was dampness, but it was dry also.

Stone tried to estimate how many days the wagon train could go without water. Every wagon carried a reserve in barrels, but horses consumed a considerable amount. Maybe three or four days.

Stone heard the tumultuous racket of the wagon train, then saw the outlines of the wagons coming through the trees.

"Is there water?" Taggart hollered from the front seat of his wagon.

"Afraid not!"

Taggart pulled back on the reins, and his horses stopped. He yanked the brake lever and jumped to the ground, hitching up his pants and walking to where Stone was standing.

"Son of a bitch," Taggart said.

He walked onto the dried-up river bottom and touched the caked muck. The other travelers climbed down from their wagons and walked on the river bottom, dismay on their faces.

"What'll we do?" asked Miss Shirley Clanton.

"We'll find water tomorrow," Taggart said, "and in the meantime, we'll stay calm. Let's pull the wagons around, folks. We'll camp here for the night."

The travelers climbed back on their wagons and moved them into a circle. Then they unhitched their horses and watered them from their barrels of reserve water. Stone and Taggart picketed their horses and lit a fire for supper.

"My experience," said Taggart, "is that a wagon train tends to get unruly when it runs out of water. Hope it doesn't come to that. You know who they're a-gonna blame if it does."

"You?"

"And you, too."

Taggart prepared their usual supper of beans and bacon and served it on tin plates.

"You gonna tell me what happened?"

Stone explained how he found the miners, shot it out with them, and left Wayne Collins trussed up like a chicken.

"You should've shot the son of a bitch," Taggart said.

They heard the sound of approaching footsteps, and it was Jason Fenwick, who'd lost substantial weight since the wagon train had left Kansas. "Captain Stone—could I speak with you alone for a moment, please?"

Stone rose and walked with Fenwick into the darkness.

"My wife and I are very grateful that you got our money back," Fenwick said, "and we'd like to give you a little present to show our appreciation." Fenwick held out a small leather pouch.

"No, that's all right," Stone said.

"It's a hundred dollars. You've earned it. It's the least we can do."

Stone hesitated. Fenwick pushed the bag into Stone's hand.

"You've saved our lives. By the way, I noticed two bullet holes in the saddlebags. What happened?"

"Accident," Stone said.

Stone walked back to Taggart and sat beside the campfire.

"What was that all about?" Taggart asked.

"Fenwick gave me a hundred dollars."

"It's not much compared to all you got back for him."

Stone pulled the pouch out of his shirt and shook it, jangling the coins. He'd be able to search for Marie full-time once the wagon train arrived in Texas.

"What are our chances of finding water tomorrow?" Stone asked.

"Hard to say. This has happened to me before, and we always found water, so I guess we'll find some sooner or later, but it ain't guaranteed. I've heard of wagon trains that ran out of water and everybody died."

Stone didn't wash before going to bed that night, because he didn't want to waste the water. He lay on the ground, his head propped up on his saddle, and wondered what death from thirst would be like. He recalled old saloon stories about people who'd gone mad from lack of water and killed each other so they could drink their blood.

13

THEY DIDN'T FIND water the next day, or the day after. The travelers became thirsty and dirty because they had to ration severely what water they had. The horses slowed their pace, their tongues hanging out of their mouths. The wagon train fell behind schedule.

Water holes and streams were dried up. Animals were found dead from thirst. Leaves withered on the branches of trees. The ground was a wasteland.

The travelers became sunken-cheeked and hollow-eyed. An atmosphere of gloom pervaded the wagon train as it rattled and clanked across the boundless horizon.

On the fifth day, Stone saw a stand of trees shimmering before him on the plains. There was supposed to be a water hole in there, and he prayed this one hadn't dried up, too. His horse rambled onward, and Stone's throat felt dry as a reed. The water in the barrels was down to the dregs. If they didn't find water soon, people would die.

The horse shuffled into the stand of trees. Stone dismounted and ran to the water hole, looked at it, and saw that it was dry.

He wanted to light a cigarette, but that'd only make him thirstier. *We're not going to make it*, he said to himself. *We're going to die like rats out here*.

The wagon train approached, and the travelers climbed

down from the wagons, advanced toward the water hole. Mike Leary knelt beside it, picked up a handful of sand, and let it seep through his fingers. Then he turned to Taggart.

"This is yer fault," he said. "You brought us here, and there ain't no water. You don't know where the hell yer goin'. Yer just an old damn goat. I don't know why I ever believed in you in the first place."

Taggart looked beat. "It ain't my fault the water hole's dry."

"You shoulda took us someplace where the water holes ain't dry. Yer the damn wagonmaster."

The travelers fixed their eyes accusingly on Taggart.

"We can dig for water," he said. "Sometimes it's jest below the surface in these dried-up water holes. Go git yer shovels. We'll give 'er a try."

None of the travelers moved. They didn't have the strength. Stone walked back to Taggart's wagon and pulled down a shovel. He returned to the water hole and took off his shirt, revealing the scar just below his ribcage on his left side. He jammed the shovel into the bottom of the water hole and began to dig.

Fatigue overtook him quickly, and his mouth was dry as cardboard. Again and again he kicked the shovel into the ground and threw the sand over his shoulder. The travelers sat around, hoping he'd strike water. But there was nothing in the bottom of the hole except dry dirt.

The Reverend Joshua McGhee stood up. "I'll spell you, Cap'n."

The hole was up to Stone's thighs. He climbed out, and the Reverend McGhee climbed in and commenced digging. Stone sat next to Taggart.

"Dry as a bone," he said.

"Don't mean nothin'," Taggart said. "Water might be just a few inches more."

Reverend McGhee continued to dig and didn't strike water. Stewart Donahue took over when McGhee was about up to his waist, and then Jason Fenwick relieved

Donahue. Tim Royster, another of the farmers, was next, and Tad Holton, the gambler, came after him.

The gambler dug until the hole was deep as his neck then threw the shovel out of the hole and climbed out. "Ain't no water in there," he said. "It's damn fool work."

Taggart jumped into the hole and got down on his hands and knees, kneading the dirt, and it was only slightly moist. They could dig another twenty feet and not find anything. He crawled out of the hole, brushed himself off, and stood before the travelers.

"I told you before we started that we might have hard times," he said. "Well, the hard times are here. The only thing to do is have trust in the Lord and keep movin'. You kin blame me for what happened, but that's not gonna git us water. The main thing is to keep goin'. There's water out there someplace. Now let's have some supper to keep our strength up, and then we'll turn in. Tomorrow's another day."

The Reverend Joshua McGhee stood up. "Do you mind if I say a little prayer?"

"Go right ahead, Reverend, and make it good."

The Reverend McGhee clasped his hands together and cleared his throat. Several of the other travelers bowed their heads, and a few of the others looked at each other as if they thought that praying was a lot of foolishness.

"Dear almighty God," said Reverend McGhee, "please help your devoted servants in our hour of need. Find us some water tomorrow, otherwise we ain't a-gonna make it to Texas. We have always revered You, O Lord. Please don't let us down. Amen."

Frank Maxsell snorted. "A lot of good that's gonna do."

"Faith can move mountains," Reverend McGhee replied.

"I ain't never seen faith move no mountain."

Frank Maxsell drew himself to his feet and spat, but no moisture came out of his mouth. He walked back to his wagon and the assembly broke up.

Stone followed Taggart to their wagon. Taggart climbed through the rear entrance and came out with tin cans. "I don't feel like lightin' no fire," he said. "Let's eat this stuff cold."

There was a can of string beans and a can of peaches. Taggart opened them and divided the contents into two bowls. Stone eagerly took his bowl and gulped down the liquid, then devoured the food. When he was finished, he felt satisfied to the point where he could smoke a cigarette.

He lit one, and Taggart smoked a cigar. They were sitting beside their wagon and the light from the coal oil lamp flickered on their faces.

"What do you think our chances are?" Stone asked.

"Can't say, but I will tell you this. If we ever get out of this alive, this is a-gonna be my last wagon train. There comes a time when a man's gotta stop what he's a-doin', and I reckon I've come to that time."

Stone smiled. "An old wagon rat like you'll never give up."

"That's where yer wrong. I've had it up to here." He drew his finger in a straight line across his throat. "I want to live a normal life. To hell with the wagon trains. Damned settlers'll have to get to Texas without me from now on."

They laid their blankets beside the wagon. Fires flickered all around the campsite, and a child was crying. One of the dogs walked up to Stone, its eyes half-closed, its legs unsteady.

"Hang on, old boy," Stone said, patting the dog's head. "We'll find water tomorrow, I bet."

The dog whined and lay down next to Stone, who sat on his blankets and finished his cigarette. Hardship would become catastrophe if they didn't find water soon.

14

THEY DIDN'T FIND water the next day or the day after. Their water barrels were empty, and they had to rely on the moisture in their canned goods.

The wagon train slowed to a crawl. The horses dragged their feet through the dry grass, their heads low to the ground, and the travelers sagged from side to side in the wagons, their eyes staring.

Another day passed, and still no water. In the morning the travelers licked the dew off the grass with the horses. Taggart was turning a sickly shade of yellow, and the flesh on his face hung down in loose folds.

"Think you can handle that team all right?" Stone asked before they hit the trail.

"Don't worry about me, young feller," Taggart wheezed. "Git on yer horse and find us some water. Maybe this'll be our lucky day."

Stone's horse traipsed forward slowly. Stone took out his map and studied the route that lay ahead. They were supposed to reach another river sometime that day, but all the other rivers and water holes had been dry, and maybe this one would be, too.

Stone drooped in the saddle, wondering if he were going to die of thirst. He felt weaker with every passing moment.

His horse plodded onward, the spring gone from his

stride, and Stone fell into a reverie of the old plantation. He was sitting on the back porch with Marie, drinking mint juleps. The sun was shining, and slaves worked in the flower garden in the backyard. Everything was wonderful, and then the movement of Stone's horse awakened him.

He peered ahead and saw the shimmering prairie stretching and undulating toward the horizon. Turning around in his saddle, he looked at the wagon train meandering behind him. The weaker ones would start dying soon.

His horse faltered. Stone climbed down to the ground and walked beside him, holding the reins in his hand.

His canteens were empty. Ahead was a brittle, brown sea of grass. The next thing was kill the animals and drink their blood. That'd keep him and the other travelers alive for another few days, and then they'd start dying one by one.

He placed one foot in front of the other as he staggered over the grassy plain. The sun glowed like a giant orb of fire in the sky. He thought his knees would give out, but he kept walking, losing all sense of time. The sun floated across the sky, and the air was hot in Stone's nostrils. He imagined fires burning all around him.

He heard eerie strains of music. Weird forms arose from the plains and danced in front of him. He saw a tall-masted ship sailing across the sky. He clenched his jaw and kept walking. Wheels of fire appeared before his eyes. He lost track of who he was. Rivulets of sweat dripped down his face, and his shirt was plastered to his back.

He wanted to drop down on the grass and go to sleep. What was the point of struggling? The joints of his knees were turning to mush. He staggered from side to side, and his horse looked at him quizzically.

Then he heard Marie's voice: "Keep going, Johnny," she said. "Don't give up now."

Stone blinked and gazed ahead. He saw Marie standing in front of him, wearing a crimson ball dress with a low-cut bodice. Her pale blond hair extended to her shoulders, and she smiled as she beckoned to him.

"You don't have much farther to go, Johnny," she said. "You'll find me if you keep trying. You can't stop now."

Stone reached out to touch her, and his fingers passed through her body. He stumbled and dropped to his knees. She touched his cheek with her cool hand and faded away.

"Come back!" he shouted.

Stone was perched on his knees, holding the reins of his horse, and there was a long line of green trees in the distance. The horse shook his head and whinnied, quickening his pace, heading for the trees. Stone caught up with him and climbed into the saddle, pulling the map out of his saddlebag.

He looked up at the sky and estimated from the position of the sun that it was mid-afternoon. Then he examined the map. It appeared that the river was straight ahead. Stone hoped it wasn't dry like all the others. The next water on the map wasn't for another fifty miles, and they'd never make it.

The horse raised his head and stumbled toward the line of trees. Stone saw something move in the corner of his right eye, but he'd hallucinated so much that day he didn't pay any attention.

He thought about the mirage of Marie. It had been so vivid, as if she'd really been there, but his mind had been playing tricks on him. "Please, God, let there be water in that riverbed."

The horse came closer to the line of trees, and Stone noticed a cooling of the air. The horse entered the forest of thick-trunked trees, and Stone peered through them eagerly for the river. He saw sandy riverbottom, and his heart sank. The river was dry, and the coolness only had come from the trees. *We're going to die*, he thought.

His horse continued to weave his way among the trees. Stone peered at the riverbed. It was sandy and covered with pebbles, but as he drew closer, he saw movement in the center.

Now he could see what had happened. The river hadn't

dried up completely! A narrow rivulet, not more than a
few feet wide, meandered through the center of the dry
riverbed. Stone yipped for joy, and the horse lurched forward, galloping toward the water.

The water glittered in the sunlight, and Stone's horse
galloped onto the sandy riverbed. Stone could hear the
soft rush of water now, and he smelled the moisture in the
air. His horse stopped in front of the water and lowered
his head into it, slurping mightily.

Stone jumped down from the saddle, dropped to his
belly, lowered his face to the crystal clear water and drank.
It was sweet and cool, and he knew he shouldn't drink too
much at first because it'd make him sick. He lay still with
his face in the water, feeling revived. They could fill up
their barrels and keep going. Stone had never been so
desperate for water in his life, but now, thank God, the
danger was over.

He heard a faint whisper behind him, and an instant
later something sharp and terrible struck the back of his
right thigh. He bellowed in pain and rolled around. An
arrow was sticking out of his thigh!

He heard a war whoop and saw figures moving among
the trees. A hail of arrows flew toward him, and he flat-
tened himself on the ground. The arrows whistled over his
head, and then Stone jumped to his feet, put his gun to
the head of his horse, and pulled the trigger. The gun fired,
and his horse went down. Stone huddled behind the dead
horse as arrows slammed into its torso.

Stone looked at his leg. The arrowhead had gone all the
way through, and blood oozed out. Stone broke off the
arrowhead, grabbed the arrow by the feathers on its shank,
and pulled it out backwards. Blood poured onto his jeans,
and the pain made him holler.

In the distance he heard gunfire and the war cries of
Indians; the wagon train was under attack! Stone pulled
his rifle out of its boot and jacked the lever. An Indian
poked his head around a tree, and Stone fired; the Indian
toppled sideways to the ground. A barrage of arrows flew

toward Stone, and he ducked behind his horse. The arrows landed with a series of thunks in the carcass.

Stone's right leg throbbed badly and he was losing blood. They hadn't fired rifles at him, which meant all they had were bows and arrows. They outnumbered him, but he had the firepower and would give them a run for their money.

The woods became silent. Stone wondered if the Indians had left to attack the greater prize, the wagon train. They'd lain their trap and sprung it perfectly.

He crouched behind his dead horse. He and it had been together for a long time, and he regretted shooting it, but there'd been no other way.

The pain in his leg was so intense he thought he'd faint. A scream erupted out of the woods before him, and five painted, half-naked Indians rushed toward him, brandishing lances, bows, and arrows. Stone raised his rifle, sighted down the barrel, and opened fire.

An Indian screamed and fell to the ground. Stone jacked the lever, took aim, and fired again. Another Indian went down. The three remaining Indians rushed toward him, hollering at the top of their lungs, and he fired again. Another brave yelped and fell.

The final two Indians jumped over the dead horse and thrust their lances at Stone. He shot one in the head, blowing out his brains, then dodged by a fraction of an inch the point of the last Indian's lance.

The Indian swung his lance around and smashed Stone in the mouth with the butt. Stone momentarily lost consciousness, dropped his rifle, and fell on his back. When he opened his eyes, he saw the Indian standing over him, pushing the lance down toward his chest. Stone rolled out at the last second and got to his knees. The Indian spread his legs and readied his lance for another try. Stone drew both his six-guns and fired. Two red dots appeared on the Indian's bare chest, and the Indian was thrown backward by the force of the bullets.

Stone dived behind his dead horse. The woods were silent, but beyond them he heard the sound of battle. It was Taggart and the others fighting for their lives, and Stone had to get to them.

He crouched behind the dead horse's back and reloaded his pistols, then opened his saddlebag and pulled out the box of ammunition for his rifle. The blood was coagulating around his wound, and it still hurt like hell.

He wondered if more Indians were in the woods. Loading the rifle, he raised his head a few inches above the horse's back, and no arrows flew at him. It seemed reasonable that they'd only sent a few Indians to kill him, while most of the war party would assault the wagon train.

Slowly he got to his feet, aiming the rifle straight ahead, and nothing moved in the foliage before him. Stone knew he'd never reach the wagon train on foot, but the dead Indians must've left their horses nearby.

He stepped over the dead Indians and limped toward the trees, expecting arrows to streak toward him at any moment. In the distance he could hear war whoops and gunfire, and he wondered how many Indians were out there.

He saw something move among the leaves and branches and dropped to his stomach, aiming his rifle at whatever he'd seen. Probing with his eyes, he saw what appeared to be the brown and chestnut coats of horses in the foliage.

He advanced cautiously in that direction, holding his rifle ready to fire. A horse snorted, and Stone knew he'd hit the mother lode. He pushed his way through the branches and saw six Indian ponies tethered to the trees. He cut the reins off one of the horses and fashioned a crude sling for his rifle, draping it across his back. Then he untethered the biggest horse, and climbed on top of it. Wheeling the horse around, he headed out of the woods.

The horse was balky with a new rider on its back. Stone put the spurs to him, and the animal leapt forward. It galloped through the woods, and Stone could see slices of the plain through the foliage. The trees thinned out, and his vision became clearer. He saw the wagon train circled on the grass, Indians riding around it, shrieking and firing arrows. A few wagons were on fire.

Gunshots peppered the air, and a cloud of gunsmoke hung over the wagon tops. Stone's horse galloped out of the woods, and Stone was on the open plain, the wind-stream billowing out his shirt. He whacked the reins over the haunches of the horse to urge it to its ultimate effort. A wall of Indians separated Stone from the wagon train, and he'd have to smash through.

It was like the war, with the same smell of danger, exalting and terrifying. He saw himself in uniform, his yellow sash around his waist, leading old Troop C against Sheridan's cavalry.

Instinctively, he reached for his cavalry saber, but it wasn't there. Looking down, he saw crossed gunbelts and blue jeans. He raised his eyes and saw not Yankee soldiers but wild savages who lusted for the white man's blood.

One of the Indians spotted Stone and shouted the warning. A group of them detached from the others, wheeled their war ponies, kicking their ponies' ribs. Yipping and yelling, they charged across the grass toward Stone.

Stone stuffed the reins in his mouth and drew his guns. The adrenaline kicked in, and he felt the old thrill of battle surge through. He drew back the hammers with his thumbs, aimed them at the Indians, and pulled the triggers. The heavy guns bucked in his hands, and one of the Indians fell off his horse. Arrows flew through the air at Stone, and he thought one of them would get him, but they zipped past, and he kept charging toward the Indians.

They were almost on top of him now, and he could see feathers in their hair and garish warpaint on their faces. They wore buckskin pants, no shirts, and their torsos were covered with warpaint. They looked like inhabitants of another world, and they wanted to tear the hair off his head.

Stone spurred the horse, and wind whistled past his old cavalry hat. He dug his teeth into the reins and fired his guns as fast as he could. One Indian was hit in the face, another in the stomach, and a third in the chest. They sagged to the side and fell off their horses, while Stone continued to trigger the guns. He shot a fourth Indian in the chest, and then the next group of Indians was only ten feet away.

Stone spurred the horse, and the horse hurled itself forward at the Indian ponies that now swerved to the side. One of the Indians yelled and lunged at Stone with his lance, but Stone batted it to the side with his left arm and fired pointblank at the Indian.

The Indian screamed, dropped the lance, and fell backward over the rump of his horse. Another Indian raised a hatchet, and Stone shot him between the eyes. The next Indian swung a warclub at Stone's head, but Stone leaned to the side, and the club whistled past harmlessly. Stone fired both guns at the Indian who fell off his galloping pony into the clouds of dust on the ground.

An Indian let loose an arrow that flew through the sleeve of Stone's shirt. Another Indian tried to dive on Stone, and Stone shot him in the heart. The Indian fell lifeless against Stone then slithered down to the ground and was trampled by horses' hooves.

Stone passed through the Indians who'd attacked him and now had to break through the Indians riding around the wagon train. He jammed one Colt into his holster and loaded the other. Then he switched and loaded the first Colt. Holding one in each hand and aiming them straight ahead, he tapped his spurs against the horse's flanks.

Strings of foam fell from the horse's lips. It'd been a wild mustang, but the Indians had captured and trained it to be a war pony. All it knew was charge. Digging its hooves into the sod, it stretched its powerful limbs and sped toward the wagon train.

The Indians were turned toward the wagon train, aiming arrows at the travelers behind the wagons, and the travelers fired a steady barrage that masked most sounds. Stone saw at least fifty Indians in front of him, and something said he'd never get through, but he had to try.

He was close enough now so that the Indians could hear his horse's pounding hooves, and he opened fire. An Indian fell off his horse, then another, then a third. The Indians turned toward him, and he was in their midst, riding hard, firing his guns.

They were taken by surprise, and he fired his Colts at

them as he broke through their ranks. Three more Indians fell off their horses in rapid succession, but a forth Indian shot an arrow into the breast of Stone's horse.

The gallant animal fell to the ground, the arrowhead in its heart, and Stone was thrown off the horse. He saw the grass coming up fast, tumbled over a few times, and landed on his stomach. The wagons were straight ahead, and an arrow slammed into the ground a few inches from his left shoulder. He sprang to his feet, dived through the air, and sailed underneath the wagon in front of him, landing beside Miss Bottom, who screamed and pointed her rifle at him.

He pushed the barrel out of the way, and she saw who he was.

"Where's Taggart?"

She pointed across the circle of wagons to the other side, and Stone saw travelers firing rifles and pistols at the Indians, while arrows flew through the air all around them. One of the travelers nearby lay on his back with an arrow sticking out of his chest. Another, whom Stone recognized as Sam Drake, the gambler, sprawled not far away with an arrow sticking out of his stomach.

Stone ran across the clearing in the middle of the wagons as arrows slammed into the sod all around him. He found Taggart behind his wagon, firing steadily at Indians who rode past and shot arrows at him and the other travelers in the vicinity.

Stone stopped beside Taggart, unslung his rifle, and raised it to his shoulder. Taggart glanced at him and nearly jumped out of his skin.

"I thought you was an Injun!" Taggart said.

Stone sighted down his rifle and drew a bead on an Indian yelling a war whoop atop his pony. Stone pulled the trigger, the rifle fired, and the Indian fell to the side. A second later an arrow smacked into the wagon a few inches from Stone's nose. Stone ducked down, and Taggart was already low, loading his rifle.

"What the hell happened to you?" Taggart asked.

"I was attacked by Indians at the river!"

"Is there water?"

"Damned right there is!"

Taggart cupped his hands around his mouth and hollered to the other travelers: "There's water straight ahead! Fight off the Injuns and you can drink it!"

A cheer arose among the travelers, then they fired and reloaded their rifles faster and with greater conviction. Stone studied the situation with the practiced eyes of a former cavalry officer. The travelers were well-protected and had superior weapons, but the Indians had superior force. Neither side had a clear-cut advantage and victory could go either way.

A flaming arrow stuck the wood on Taggart's wagon, and seconds later tongues of flame licked up toward the canvas.

"Cover me!" Stone said.

Stone leapt up onto the seat of the wagon and nearly fell over because his wounded leg didn't hold him up as well as he'd thought it would. He righted himself and reached for the flaming arrow, yanking it out of the wood and dropping it to the ground. An Indian screamed and a second later landed on top of Stone, raising his hatchet in the air, preparing to bury it in Stone's head, but Taggart shot the Indian in the ribs, and the Indian slid off Stone's back.

Stone kicked the Indian off the wagon and jumped to the ground beside Taggart. There was no time to say thank you, there were too many Indians to kill.

"Help!"

Stone saw a group of Indians streaming between the wagons where Stewart and Martha Donahue were with their children. An Indian raised the war club in his hand and brought it down on Stewart Donahue's head, and Donahue collapsed onto the ground. Stone ran toward them across the open ground, holding his rifle in his hands.

One of the Indians grabbed Martha Donahue by the hair, and she shrieked like a madwoman. Stone dropped his rifle and pulled out both his Colts, firing from the waist as he charged in.

The Indian who held Martha Donahue's hair was shot

through the neck. An expression of surprise came over his face, and he fell on top of her. Three other Indians, carrying a lance, a tomahawk, and a war club, shouted war cries and rushed toward Stone.

He dropped to one knee and picked his shots, firing from left to right. He shot down two of the Indians, and took aim at the third with the pistol in his right hand. The Indian was almost on top of him, swinging the war club in the air, and Stone pulled the trigger.

Click! The Indian swung his war club at Stone's head, and Stone fired the pistol in his left hand, but that pistol jammed. Stone grabbed the Indian's wrist with both his hands, spun around, and threw the Indian over his shoulder. The Indian landed on his back, and in a second bounced back to his feet. Then a shot rang out, and the Indian grimaced. There was a hole in his kidney, and blood spewed out of it. He took two steps toward Stone then fell to his knees, paused a moment, and dropped onto his face.

Stone looked in the direction of the shot. He saw young Cornelius Donahue, a smoking rifle in his hand. Stone reloaded his pistols as quickly as he could. He could see no more Indians within the defensive perimeter.

Cornelius Donahue knelt over his mother and tried to rouse her. Stone grabbed him by the shirt and pulled him to his feet. "Fire your rifle at the Indians!"

Stone pushed Cornelius into a position behind his dead father's wagon, and the boy jacked the lever, took aim at an Indian on a war pony, and shot him out of the saddle. Stone turned around and ran across the expanse of grass toward Taggart on the other side.

Stone picked up his rifle in the middle of the clearing and continued his headlong rush toward Taggart. Several wagons were on fire, and bodies lay everywhere. A steady fusillade was maintained by the travelers, and the women and children were out there with the men, all firing rifles, pistols, and even derringers. Stone saw Homer Hodge, one of the dudes from the East atop his wagon, slapping a fire with his hat, when suddenly an arrow appeared in his back. Hodge froze for a moment, silhouetted against the clear blue sky, then fell backward to the ground.

Taggart was hunched behind his wagon, loading and firing, and beside him was a box of ammunition. "Aim steady and keep firing!" he hollered. "The only way to keep 'em off us is to keep firing!"

Stone took a position beside Taggart, rested his rifle on the wagon, took aim, and fired at an Indian about to shoot an arrow. The bullet hit the Indian in the shoulder, spinning him around on his pony, and the arrow soared into the air high over the wagon train.

Stone jacked the lever, took aim at another Indian, led him a bit, and fired. The Indian pitched forward onto the mane of his horse, and blood made a red ribbon down the Indian's side.

Stone heard a *thunk* sound beside him, and Taggart gasped. Stone turned to look at Taggart, and Taggart was dropping to the ground, an arrow sticking out of his chest. Stone let go of his rifle and tried to catch Taggart.

Taggart dropped to a sitting position, an expression of bewilderment on his face. His hat had fallen off and he looked like a sick old man. Stone kneeled beside him and tried to hold him up. Taggart's shirt was rapidly becoming drenched with bright red blood.

"I'm a goner," Taggart whispered.

He became dead weight in Stone's arms, and Stone knew the old wagonmaster would never see Texas again. Taggart's eyes were wide open and staring, and his blood soaked into Stone's clothes. Stone gently laid him on the ground.

A blood-curdling scream rent the air behind Stone. He turned around and saw an Indian with a hatchet in his hand, warpaint all over his body, wearing a breechcloth and moccasins. The Indian swung his hatchet at Stone's head.

Stone picked up his rifle and raised it to block the blow. The hatchet slammed against the rifle, and Stone felt the great strength of the Indian. The Indian raised his knee to kick Stone in the groin, and Stone pivoted to the side, receiving the blow on his outer thigh. The Indian screamed his battle cry once more, dropped his hatchet, and grabbed Stone's rifle, trying to pull it out of Stone's hand.

Stone was nearly jerked off his feet by the power of the Indian who was shorter than Stone, but nearly as wide. They grappled desperately for possession of the rifle, pushing and pulling, trying to trip each other, and then the Indian spit in Stone's face, trying to unnerve him.

Stone didn't get unnerved. He yanked mightily, and the Indian hooked one foot behind the back of Stone's wounded leg. Stone lost his balance, but didn't let the rifle go.

He fell to the ground, and the Indian dropped on top of him. They rolled around in the dust, fighting for the rifle. Stone realized he couldn't get the rifle away from the Indian, and the Indian couldn't take it from him. Stone reached down into his boot and pulled out his knife, but the Indian saw what he'd done and grabbed his wrist as Stone brought the knife up.

The Indian bucked and twisted, and Stone held on for dear life. The Indian was a wild man, all muscle, sinew, and bone, and Stone had been weakened by loss of blood. His face and the Indian's were just inches apart as they contended with each other, and the Indian spat on him again. Stone got mad and spat on the Indian, and the Indian blinked. Stone knew the man with superior strength would win the fight, and somehow he had to suck up his remaining reserves.

Stone and the Indian tossed about on the ground, each trying to gain an advantage over the other, and Stone could hear other Indians running wild inside the wagon train. The Indian leaned his head forward and tried to bite Stone's nose, but Stone turned his rifle loose and pressed his big hand against the Indian's face, pushing it backward, but the Indian had the rifle all to himself now and tried to clobber Stone over the head with it.

Stone twisted his knife hand loose and jabbed it with all his strength into the Indian's stomach. The Indian screamed and let go of the rifle. Stone pulled out the knife and stuck it in again, ripping across the Indian's belly. The Indian screamed and fell to the ground.

Stone picked up the rifle and got to his feet. Two Indians charged out of the smoke and dust, one armed with a lance, the other carrying a war club. Stone leveled the rifle, fired a shot, and hit the Indian with the lance, then swung the rifle around and smashed the butt into the face of the Indian carrying the war club.

Another Indian jumped onto Stone's back with a loud shriek. One of the Indian's hands grasped the front of Stone's shirt, and the other held a long-bladed knife that he thrust toward Stone's throat.

Stone grabbed the Indian's wrist with both hands, halting it in midair, while the Indian wrapped his legs around Stone, grasping Stone's throat with his free hand. Stone brought his elbow back hard into the Indian's stomach, and the Indian loosened his grip on Stone momentarily. Stone twisted around, backfisted the Indian, and the Indian dropped dazed to the ground. Stone drew his knife and cut the Indian's throat.

Stone heard Alice McGhee scream behind him. He turned around, pulled out his guns, and jumped over the body of the dead Indian, running toward a horde of half-naked Indians surrounding the Reverend Joshua McGhee and his family.

The McGhees were armed with rifles, but the Indians outnumbered them and were about to swarm over them when Stone charged into their midst and opened fire. Bullets flew through the air like angry hornets, and the Indians were cut down by the combined firepower. They lay in a bloody mound around the McGhee family, and the McGhees hastily loaded their weapons for the next assault.

Stone heard a cry for help from the other side of the wagon train. He saw a group of Indians inside the perimeter attacking the Fenwick family. Stone rushed toward them, and every time he took a step, he had to hop because of his stiffening leg. The atmosphere was filled with dust, smoke, yells, and Stone pulled the triggers of his pistols, firing a barrage at the Indians.

They shrieked and twisted in pain as the bullets ripped into them. Stone smashed one in the face with the barrel of his Colt and kicked another in the stomach. A third Indian charged Stone, poising his lance for a throw, but Stone aimed his guns and pulled the triggers.

Click went the pistol in his right hand, and then, a split second later, the pistol in his left hand went *click*, too. Both had gone empty at the same time, and Stone's worst nightmare came true. He thought he was going to die. The Indian threw his lance and Stone dived to the side. The lance missed his ear by a half-inch, and Stone landed again on the ground. The Indian took a war club from his belt, raised it, and made an ululating sound with his mouth as he leapt toward Stone, swinging the club down.

Stone grabbed the Indian's wrist with his left hand and whacked him in the face with the Colt in his right hand. The barrel of the gun laid the Indian's scalp open to the bone, and the Indian fell to the ground with a skull fracture.

Indian battle cries pierced the air to the right of Stone, and he saw two more Indians charging toward him. One carried a lance and the other a tomahawk. Stone holstered his empty pistols, picked up a fallen Indian's war club, and ran to meet them.

The Indian on the left pushed his lance toward Stone's belly, but Stone deflected it with a sideways swipe of his arm, crashing his war club into the Indian's head, and then on the backswing, struck the other Indian in the face. Both Indians toppled at Stone's feet, but more Indians screeched like wild animals a short distance away.

Stone turned in their direction and saw three Indians charging him. He picked up a tomahawk lying on the ground, and now was armed with a war club and a tomahawk. One of the three Indians took one look at Stone, faltered, turned around, and ran in the opposite direction, but the other two Indians kept coming, murderous gleams in their eyes.

Stone waded into them, wielding his war club and tomahawk. One of the Indians carried a knife and managed to cut open Stone's arm before Stone buried the tomahawk in his skull. The other Indian swung his war club at Stone's head, and Stone couldn't pull his tomahawk loose from the first Indian's head. He let it go, leaned backward, and the Indian's war club scraped the end of his nose. Stone swung his war club sideways, but the Indian ducked, and Stone's war club passed over the Indian's head.

Stone and the Indian circled each other, holding their war clubs ready as fighting raged around them. Then Stone and the Indian rushed each other at the same time, swinging their war clubs at each other's heads. They both reached up, catching each other's wrists, and now they were locked together tightly, glaring into each other's bloodshot eyes.

The Indian grunted and pushed, but Stone held his ground. Then Stone pushed, and the Indian gave ground. Stone had no resistance and went stumbling forward. The Indian stepped out of the way and held out his foot. Stone tripped and fell to the ground.

The Indian was on him in an instant, raising his war club for the death blow. Suddenly there was the explosion of a rifle, and the Indian's head shattered. The Indian toppled over onto his side, and Stone was splattered with blood. He sat up and saw Alice McGhee, her dress in tatters and a smoking rifle in her hands.

Stone didn't have time to thank her. He jumped to his feet, yanked out his pistols, and loaded them quickly.

"Watch out!" shouted Alice.

Stone looked up and saw a crowd of Indians speeding toward him. Two had rifles and one a pistol that they'd taken from a dead traveler. Stone went into a gunfighter's crouch and opened fire. The Indians returned his fire but were unfamiliar with the weapons, and their bullets flew harmlessly over Stone's head.

Stone wasn't unfamiliar with his weapons, and his fusillade blew down the front rank of the Indians. He continued firing, nearly choking on his own thick gunsmoke, while Alice shot at the Indians from her position slightly behind him and to his right.

There was so much smoke it was hard to see what was going on, but Stone had a sense that the Indians were dropping to the ground. Then two Indians burst through the smoke. Both carried lances poised ready to throw at Stone's heart.

Stone dropped to one knee and pulled the triggers of his pistols, while Alice fired her rifle. The Indians were torn apart by the bullets and toppled to the ground.

Stone thumbed fresh cartridges into his guns and got to his feet, expecting more Indians to rush him. But no Indians came. They were running away, heading for their horses. Stone was taut as a guitar string, his teeth clenched, holding his pistols ready to fire again. His heart beat like a tom-tom. He ran toward the nearest opening between wagons and saw Indians riding off toward the hills, their elbows and legs flapping up and down.

Stone was aware of somebody beside him. He turned and saw Alice McGhee, the bodice of her dress torn and half of her left breast showing. Her eyes were glazed with horror.

"Are you all right?" Stone asked.

She collapsed at his feet. She had no wounds, and he figured she'd passed out due to the strain. Glancing around, he saw travelers sitting, laying their rifles down.

"Hold your positions!" Stone shouted to them. "Load your rifles! The Indians might come back!"

The travelers dragged themselves off the ground and hunted for their extra ammunition. They loaded their rifles and positioned themselves behind the wagons, waiting for the Indians to mount another attack.

Stone reloaded his rifle and gazed onto the plains. The Indians were gone, but they might come back. He wiped his forehead with the palm of his hand. He was thirsty and hungry, aware of cuts and bruises all over his body, and his leg ached fiercely.

Stone remembered Taggart, killed by an Indian arrow. A deep sadness came over him as he walked across the clearing to Taggart's wagon. He saw Taggart lying on the ground next to one of the wheels, the arrow sticking out of his chest. Taggart's head was covered with blood—the Indians had scalped him.

Stone kneeled down next to Taggart, picked up his hat, and covered his head. "You said this was going to be your last wagon train, and you were right."

Stone got to his feet and knew he was in charge of the wagon train now. He raised his rifle, leaned against the front of the wagon and looked out at the plains. No Indians were in sight.

Stone looked at the position of the sun in the sky. It was low on the horizon, and soon night would come. Stone rolled himself a cigarette; his nerves were jangled. There'd been moments when he'd thought he was going to die, but he hadn't died. Yankees had been ordinary human beings, but Indians were alien creatures who attacked out of nowhere, fought like fiends, and disappeared.

He and the travelers waited for the Indians to attack again, but the Indians didn't come. The sun sank lower on the horizon and dipped behind the hills. Darkness came to the plains, and the wounded moaned. Stone had heard that Indians usually didn't attack at night and hoped that was true.

Footsteps came to him, and he turned around. It was a group of the travelers, led by the Reverend Joshua McGhee. McGhee took off his hat as he looked down at the dark form of Taggart lying on the ground.

"Guess yer in charge now. We was thinkin' that we should move on to the river. We're awful thirsty."

"Load your dead and wounded onto the wagons," Stone said, "and move out when I give the word."

The travelers returned to their wagons. Stone lowered the tailgate of Taggart's wagon and lifted Taggart off the ground, carrying him to the wagon, laying him in back.

Stone rolled another cigarette. It was dark, and nobody could see him. He bent his head and permitted himself to weep for the brave old man.

15

In THE DARK of night, the wagon train moved toward the river. Everyone who could use a rifle held one in case the Indians attacked. The wagons rumbled among the trees, and the travelers couldn't wait to drink deeply of the cool clear water, but they had to be careful. The fight with the Indians had made a deep impression on them.

The men set up a defense perimeter, while the women and children drank. Then canteens of water were brought to the men on guard. Meals were prepared, and the moon bathed the scene in a ghostly glow. Stone walked to his old horse lying dead beside the river. He kneeled next to the horse and thought of all the country they'd seen together. The horse had been a good one, loyal and strong. Stone wished he'd treated him better, but it was too late now.

Alice McGhee approached, carrying a roll of bandages and a pair of scissors. "Want me to look at your leg?"

Stone lay on the ground and she cut open his pants, exposing the wound.

"Doesn't look infected."

A canteen was hanging from a protuberance on the wagon. Alice took it and washed the wound, while Stone grit his teeth and felt her cool hands on his skin.

"Do you think the Indians will come back?"

"Don't know."

She tied a bandage around his leg, snipped off the end with the scissors, and tied a bow.

"Finished."

"You'd better get some rest. We'll all have to be up early tomorrow."

She hesitated, as if she wanted to talk.

"Are you all right?"

Her eyes became watery, and she let out a sob. He placed his hand on her shoulder.

"You were a good soldier today," he told her. "Don't give up now."

Half the travelers went to sleep, while the other half stood guard. Stone limped around the defense perimeter, telling travelers where to position themselves, urging them to stay awake. They gazed out onto the plains, hearing the calls of birds and chirpings of crickets, and wondered if Indians were out there someplace, preparing to attack.

The guard shifts changed, and Stone stayed awake, making sure the new guards understood their duties. Then he returned to Taggart's wagon and crawled into his blankets. He closed his eyes and fell asleep almost instantly.

Everyone was up before dawn, holding their rifles and peering onto the plains, waiting anxiously for the Indians to attack. Stone roamed about the wagons, checking the defense, trying to raise everybody's morale.

"You beat them yesterday!" he said. "You can beat them again if you maintain a steady volley of fire!"

The sun rose higher in the sky, and the Indians didn't come. The settlers grew restless. Some lay on the ground and tried to rest, but Stone ordered them back to their positions. They had to be vigilant if they wanted to stop the Indians.

Women prepared lunch while the others maintained their positions behind the wagons. The travelers ate with their rifles close at hand. Throughout the rest of the afternoon, they waited for the Indians to attack again.

In late afternoon, Stone suspected the Indians had gone. The travelers filled their water barrels and dug a big hole in the ground, then carried the stiff bodies of their loved ones to the hole and laid them inside. Stone and Reverend McGhee lowered Taggart in last.

"I'd like to say a few words for the repose of their souls," Reverend McGhee said.

The group of travelers stood around the hole, and the men removed their hats. Some of the travelers continued to stand guard, holding their rifles in their hands.

"Lord," said Reverend McGhee, "please accept into Your loving arms the souls of these brave men and women who died fighting the heathen savage. Have mercy on them, bless them, and keep them close to You always. Amen." He looked at Stone. "Care to say anything, Captain?"

"Let's hitch up our wagons and get out of here."

They filled the mass grave with dirt and placed a wooden cross on top. Then they formed up the wagon train. Cornelius Donahue agreed to drive Taggart's old wagon, and a few wagons had to be left behind because their owners had been killed.

They left the extra wagons on the plains for whomever might be able to use them. Stone sat on the spirited horse he'd taken from Hank Owsley and moved his arm forward.

"Wagons ho!"

The wagon train moved forward, wheels creaking and carriages rocking from side to side. The sun was an orange and red ball of fire dropping toward the horizon. Some of the wagons were charred from the flaming arrows of the Indians, and the travelers sat inside, their faces grim, and many were bandaged. They'd fought for the land and now would never give it up.

Guards took their positions on the flanks. Stone galloped forward to take the point, leaving Reverend McGhee behind as second in command.

Stone slowed down his horse when he was in position, and looked back at the wagons winding their way over the grass in the glow of the setting sun. He scanned the hills and basins, looking for signs of Indians. Maybe they were beaten, back in their teepees licking their wounds, or maybe they were behind the next hill, massed for an attack.

He pulled his hat low over his eyes and settled into the saddle, peering ahead. The wagon train stretched behind him over the plains as it rolled onward toward Texas.

A special offer for people who enjoy reading the best Westerns published today. If you enjoyed this book, subscribe now and get...

TWO FREE WESTERNS!
A $5.90 VALUE—NO OBLIGATION

If you enjoyed this book and would like to read more of the very best Westerns being published today, you'll want to subscribe to True Value's Western Home Subscription Service. If you enjoyed the book you just read and want more of the most exciting, adventurous, action packed Westerns, subscribe now.

TWO FREE BOOKS

When you subscribe, we'll send you your first month's shipment of the newest and best 6 Westerns for you to preview. With your first shipment, two of these books will be yours as our introductory gift to you absolutely FREE, regardless of what you decide to do.

Special Subscriber Savings

As a True Value subscriber all regular monthly selections will be billed at the low subscriber price of just $2.45 each. That's at least a savings of $3.00 each month below the publishers price. There is never any shipping, handling or other hidden charges. What's more there is no minimum number of books you must buy, you may return any selection for full credit and you can cancel your subscription at any time. A TRUE VALUE!

Mail the coupon below

To start your subscription and receive 2 FREE WESTERNS, fill out the coupon below and mail it today. We'll send you your first shipment which includes 2 FREE BOOKS as soon as we receive it.

Mail To: True Value Home Subscription Services, Inc.
P.O. Box 5235
120 Brighton Road
Clifton, New Jersey 07015-5235

557-73307

YES! I want to start receiving the very best Westerns being published today. Send me my first shipment of 6 Westerns for me to preview FREE for 10 days. If I decide to keep them, I'll pay for just 4 of the books at the low subscriber price of $2.45 each; a total of $9.80 (a $17.70 value). Then each month I'll receive the 6 newest and best Westerns to preview Free for 10 days. If I'm not satisfied I may return them within 10 days and owe nothing. Otherwise I'll be billed at the special low subscriber rate of $2.45 each; a total of $14.70 (at least a $17.70 value) and save $3.00 off the publishers price. There are never any shipping, handling or other hidden charges. I understand I am under no obligation to purchase any number of books and I can cancel my subscription at any time, no questions asked. In any case the 2 FREE books are mine to keep.

Name _____

Address _____ Apt. # _____

City _____ State _____ Zip _____

Telephone # _____

Signature _____
(if under 18 parent or guardian must sign)

Terms and prices subject to change. Orders subject to acceptance by True Value Home Subscription Services, Inc.

SONS OF TEXAS

The exciting saga of America's Lone Star state!

TOM EARLY

Texas, 1816. A golden land of opportunity for anyone who dared to stake a claim in its destiny...and its dangers...

___	SONS OF TEXAS	0-425-11474-0/$3.95
___	SONS OF TEXAS #2: THE RAIDERS	0-425-11874-6/$3.95
___	SONS OF TEXAS #3: THE REBELS	0-425-12215-8/$3.95

Look for each new book in the series!

Check book(s). Fill out coupon. Send to:

BERKLEY PUBLISHING GROUP
390 Murray Hill Pkwy., Dept. B
East Rutherford, NJ 07073

NAME_____

ADDRESS_____

CITY_____

STATE_____ZIP_____

PLEASE ALLOW 6 WEEKS FOR DELIVERY. PRICES ARE SUBJECT TO CHANGE WITHOUT NOTICE.

POSTAGE AND HANDLING:
$1.00 for one book, 25¢ for each additional. Do not exceed $3.50.

BOOK TOTAL $_____

POSTAGE & HANDLING $_____

APPLICABLE SALES TAX $_____
(CA, NJ, NY, PA)

TOTAL AMOUNT DUE $_____

PAYABLE IN US FUNDS.
(No cash orders accepted.)

203b